KILTY
CONSCIENCE

LOVE. INTRIGUE. POOFY DRESSES.

Amy Vansant

ISBN-13: 9780998130859
Library of Congress: 2017907852

Vansant Creations, LLC / Amy Vansant
Annapolis, MD
http://www.AmyVansant.com

Cover art by Steven Novak
Copy editing by Carolyn Steele.

DEDICATION

For the fans who keep me writing and help me name my characters when they're being mysterious.

CONTENTS

CHAPTER ONE

Brochan watched her from a distance, her dark hair streaming behind her as she galloped across the glen upon a chestnut mare.

Like a princess from a fairytale.

Over her shoulder, she flashed a smiled.

He urged on his mount.

Though he found himself increasingly fascinated with the other rider, their horses weren't fond of each other. His gelding nipped at her mare's neck when they rode side by side, so he'd fallen back.

What a happy accident to gain such a lovely view.

Reaching a lone oak, she reined in her horse and dismounted. He joined her, leaving his gelding on the opposite side of the great oak so the horses didn't antagonize one another. Both creatures dipped their heads to graze. No friends or foes when there was grass to be eaten.

The woman stared across the glen at Edinburgh castle, her back to him.

"We should return. People will blether," he said.

She glanced at him, the light in her eyes dancing with mischief. "You worry too much. No one saw us. And it's no matter. I'm from *America*. Here, they already think I'm *scandalous* for one reason or another."

He smiled and rested a hand on her hip, leaning close to whisper in her ear. "But it's mah duty tae protect yer honor."

She spun and placed her hands on his chest. "Then I have nothing to fear, do I?"

She tilted back her head to smile at him and he kissed her. He couldn't not.

"Look whit ye made me dae," he said.

She slipped away from him, laughing. Patting her mare, she fussed with the bridle. "It's eighteen thirty three. Times are changing."

He frowned.

Eighteen thirty three?

"Catriona, whit did ye say?"

He reached out to touch her shoulder and she faced him, scowling. "What did you call me?"

Something about her had changed. He withdrew his hand and wiped his eyes. Refocusing, he saw her staring at him, but her features remained blurry.

"Somethin's wrong," he said.

She put her hands on her hips. "You know my name. Say it."

"Ah dinnae ken—"

"*Say it.*"

He took a step back, a hissing building in his head.

"Say my *name*," she repeated stepping towards him. The light of the setting sun struck something in her hand and it flashed.

She was holding a knife.

Stumbling back, his heel struck the base of the oak

and he fell against it. He put his hands on his ears as the growing din in his head roared like a storm-tossed ocean trapped in his skull.

"Mah head. Somethin's wrong. Ah—"

He dropped to his knees.

She approached, standing over him.

"Say my name."

There has to be a way to make the noise stop.

"Say my name."

She was nearly upon him.

The noise became unbearable and he screamed.

"Fiona!"

Broch awoke sitting in a strange bed in an unfamiliar room. A low, snorty growl sounded beside him and, recognizing it as a less-deafening version of the sound in his dream, he turned towards it.

In another small bed, separated from his own by a small table, Catriona snored.

"Did you say something?'" she mumbled, her eyes fluttering open.

"Na," he said, laying back down.

She rolled over and her breathing grew heavy.

Broch remembered where they were. The drapes of their Tennessee hotel were drawn, but through the sliver where they met, he could see it was still dark.

He whispered the name to himself to see how it felt on his tongue.

"Fiona."

CHAPTER TWO

Catriona retrieved her phone to call Peter Roseum, a Parasol Pictures work-colleague.

Peter was ideally suited for his job at the movie studio. In the pursuit of perfection, Hollywood talent never ran out of ways to injure themselves. Peter saw strange and ghastly things on a daily basis, and then rolled to lunch without a dent in his appetite. He'd seen things that kept *her* off the feedbag for a week.

Peter Roseum never shared horror stories with the press, earning him the name Doctor *No-see-um*—the name Catriona now pressed in her speed dial. She had to lay a little groundwork before heading back to Hollywood.

"Hey, where are you?" said Noseeum, answering.

He'd never *not* answered her call. She wasn't sure he slept.

"Tennessee," she said, strolling down the hotel hallway.

"Tennessee? What's *that*?"

"It's a state. Believe it or not, there's life outside of California. Whole oceans even."

He sniffed. "There be dragons."

She chuckled. Noseeum came from a wealthy Southern California family and, other than the few years he spent at a Caribbean-based medical school, she didn't think he'd ever deigned to leave the Golden State. She didn't have enough battery life left on her phone to convince him Tennessee had its own charms.

She plowed ahead.

"Remember that guy I found passed out on the lot?"

"The naked Highlander I helped you stuff into your Jeep? Yes, I vaguely recall."

"Yeah, well, his name is Brochan and he didn't turn out to be background talent."

"No? I saw his *background talent* and it looked pretty talented to me. If you like that sort of thing."

"Ha. No, Pete, that naked butt was an omen that my whole world was about to change. He was the straw that sent the camel crashing to his knees. The Book of Revelations read by Sean Connery on a bender."

"Boy. That's a lot of things for a naked butt to be."

She sighed. All she wanted to do was tell *someone* everything that had happened to her over the last few days. How her week had barreled like an eighteen wheeler with the brake lines cut. How she'd found a gorgeous Highlander on a Hollywood movie set. How she'd been kidnapped by a man with a removable face. How her adoptive father, Sean, believed both he and Brochan had traveled from eighteenth century Scotland to modern day California...and how Sean was pretty sure that Brochan was his son.

How do you tell someone your adopted father and the stranger you found passed out on the studio lot are a pair of time-travelers?

You don't.

That information wasn't something she could share with even a human-vault like Noseeum. He might be sworn by his medical oath to commit her. Anyway, she didn't want him thinking she'd lost her mind.

The worst part was that Noseeum was so well trained, he'd never pry. She needed him to *pry* so she could unburden herself and then *blame him for prying.* Women-friends understood things like that. Noseeum didn't get it.

She huffed. "You're useless."

"Where did that come from?"

"If you were a woman, you'd know."

"Right. I'll be sure to work on that. So, did you call just to insult me?"

Catriona sighed. "No. Sorry. Since Broch showed up, I'm a little off-kilter."

"No pun intended."

"*Kilt*er. I get it. Funny."

"I have my moments."

"Anyway, I wanted to let you know that Broch's working with me now. If he needs anything give it to him."

"Hey now. I'm not that easy."

Catriona ignored him and barreled on, her agitation piquing. "Can you believe Sean *hired* Broch? He just dropped him into the job I spent *years* earning."

"Life is so unfair."

"It is, Pete, it really is. I mean sure, Broch's probably Sean's son, but still—"

"What?"

"Broch. He's more than likely Sean's son."

Catriona held her breath. *Is Noseeum prying? Is he giving me an in? Can I tell him everything and get this off my chest?*

It occurred to her that there'd been nothing but silence on the other end of the line for some time.

"Pete, did you hear me? Broch is Sean's son."

Noseeum grunted an affirmative. "Got it. So, are we done here or...?"

Son of a—

"Almost. I called to tell you about Broch and let you know Sean was shot. Long story."

"What? Is he okay?"

Catriona was touched to hear genuine concern in Noseeum's voice. "He's fine."

"You're calling me for medical advice? This mythical Tennessee place doesn't have doctors? Is he lying there at your feet, bleeding?"

Catriona rolled her eyes. *There it is. The great white snark had returned.*

"No, idiot. He was shot a few days ago during a job."

She paused to test if Pete would ask for more information.

He didn't.

Bastard. I'll never get him to pry his way into my personal problems if he won't even pry into a shooting.

Convinced the conversational ball was firmly back in her court, she continued.

"When Sean gets back to L.A., I want you to swing by and tell him his wounds are much worse than they look."

"Huh?"

"You know him. He's going to act like it's a papercut. I want him to take it easy."

"Oh, gotcha. No problem."

"And if he ever tells you to lie to *me* like I'm asking you to lie to him, you be sure to tell *me* the truth, okay?"

"Always."

She offered him the opportunity to ignore her final, exasperated sigh and said her goodbyes.

Today I'll put the screws to Sean. Hopped-up on pain medication, he'd let it slip that she, too, might be of time-traveling stock. Shot or not, she needed to find out what he'd meant. He couldn't just *say* things like that. It was like telling someone, *oh, by the way, there's a chance you can fly* and then wandering off without explanation.

She'd tried to make Sean talk at the hospital, but he'd clammed up.

She closed her eyes and tried to think.

I have no memories of ever wearing a kilt.

Hm. Speaking of kilts...

She turned and strode back up the hallway of their Knoxville hotel to their room. She'd left the door ajar, and entered to find Broch shirtless and kilted, his torso a muscly-terrain of man-flesh. It appeared that after his usual hour-long shower, he'd foregone his new jeans and returned to his tartan.

She ogled the six taut hills of his stomach and released a tiny, involuntary groan.

"Are ye well?" he asked, toweling his hair.

Her attention snapped to his eyes.

"What? Yes, I'm fine. Why?"

He shrugged and turned, his shoulder length hair dancing across his broad muscular back.

She sighed.

The previous night they'd both been so tired from their ordeal saving Sean from an age-old enemy, that they'd both fallen asleep without investigating where their bodies might lead them.

Hm. She was sick of spending half her time confused and frustrated by Broch's very existence, and the other half longing to read his body like braille. It didn't help her visceral *need* to resent him for co-opting her job and her father, that he was so damn charming and easy-going.

And hot. So, so *hot.*

Broch's sense of whimsy made her doubt that he really *was* from the past. She'd never pictured eighteenth-century men being so jocular. She thought they march around all day killing boars and slamming together mugs of mead, toasting the hunt. Until Broch appeared, she'd only imagined Highlanders grunting, painting their faces blue and scratching themselves.

She put a hand on her hip and cocked her head, studying his kilt. He turned again and her eyes locked on the little tuft of hair leading from his belly button into the kilt.

What do people call that? The happy trail?

She saw he was staring at her and searched for a good reason why her focus had perched where it did.

"You're not wearing your big-boy pants," she said.

"Whit?"

"You're in your kilt again."

"Aye. Ah dinnae see how come ah should carry mah kilt when ah kin wear it as t'was intended."

Right. Not having his kilt with him was like asking a Boy Scout to leave his pocket knife at home.

She had to admit, Brochan *did* wear a kilt with a flair no modern-day man could muster. He did *everything* with certain swaggering-yet-adorable confidence. It wasn't the obnoxious confidence of a *cocky* man. More the conviction of a little boy who had yet to discover the world didn't always work in his favor.

Broch fumbled with the in-room coffee maker and she watched him pour water through the empty filter area, directly on to the cold burner.

As the water splashed on his bare belly, he spat something in another language she felt confident was a profanity.

She smirked.

The coffee machine isn't falling for his charms.

He bit the corner of a single-serving coffee bag to tear it open and it exploded, showering a three-foot radius with dark roast dust.

She chortled.

"Stop yer laughing." He frowned at the smattering of coffee on his bare feet. Emptying the grains that remained in the pack into the filter, he refilled the coffee pot and this time poured it in the correct receptacle.

But for the coffee sprinkles, his feet looked fantastic. The previous night she'd introduced him to the joys of toe-nail clippers after catching him trimming with the steak knife left from room service. He'd nearly split with delight while using the tool, and insisted she let him clip her toenails as well.

"You know, you could have asked me how it works," she said, motioning to the coffee maker.

He sniffed. "Ah'll figure it oot."

"But see, that's the thing. You don't *have* to figure it out. *I can show you.*"

He set his jaw. "Lassie, if ah'm aff tae be staying 'ere ah'm needin' tae figure things oot."

She giggled at how serious he'd grown over the workings of a Mr. Coffee. "You think if you solve how to use that machine, it will provide you with life skills for the future?"

He snorted. "*Life skills.* Ye invent more words in a day than ah've known mah entire life."

Broch felt the burner. His expression confirmed what she already knew—it was cold. He'd not turned on the machine.

Muttering, he found the on-button and pressed it. No light flashed. Spotting the unplugged electrical cord, he became engrossed by the prongs on it, holding it against various parts of the coffee machine, puzzling where to insert it.

"Look. I'd like to have coffee sometime *this* century, so how about I make it?"

Broch scowled. "Fine. But ah willnae watch."

He stepped aside and turned his back to her, crossing his arms over his beefy chest.

Catriona brushed what coffee she could save from the counter and dumped it into the filter. As she plugged in the machine, she experienced the feeling of being watched. Broch had stationed himself in front of a mirror and observed her every movement in it. When she caught his stare, he looked away and twisted his body to the left as if that proved he hadn't been watching.

"Och, tis nae my fault they put a keekin' glass here. Dinnae mean ah'm keekin' at *ye*."

She nodded, trying to appear as solemn as possible. "Of course not."

"Ye tell't me never to keek at ye."

"That's right. We have a keek-free relationship now."

She turned on the machine. As the switch light blinked to life, she heard Broch grunt. It was the sound someone might make while kicking themselves for not noticing the obvious.

Brewing didn't get far before Broch shouted *Ha!* and pointed to the machine. Brown, speckled water bubbled from the top, spilling to the counter at an alarming rate.

Catriona yelped and fumbled to stop the machine

from percolating its mess. It stopped with a final hiss, and she squinted in Broch's direction.

"Did you try and put coffee in it without the filter? You must have blocked the hole with coffee and it backed up."

He pursed his lips as if offended that she'd ask such a question. "Ah dinnae ken whit that means but *nae.*"

Catriona gathered her things. "Let's get coffee at the hospital."

Broch winced. "The hospital coffee?"

She had to agree with his assessment. "You're right. The hospital coffee was pretty bad. We can grab some downstairs on the way."

Broch took a step toward the door and she reached out to put a palm on his chest, stopping his progress. Ignoring the heat of his flesh beneath her fingertips and the fascinating ridges of his pectorals, she found the strength to hold fast.

"No shirt, no shoes, no service," she said.

"Whit?"

"You have to wear a *shirt* in public. Remember? We talked about this."

He glanced down at his naked torso. "Aye."

He grabbed a white t-shirt they'd bought at the hotel store the day before and slipped it over his head. It had "Knox Vul" printed on it in large black letters, mimicking the way the locals pronounced the name of their city.

She crossed her arms against her chest and tongued the side of her cheek, studying his ensemble.

A novelty tee and a kilt. Would it be better to let him head out shirtless and remove all doubt that he's a loon?

She decided to let it go. He passed her and moved into the hallway, beaming with manly swagger.

At least he wears it well.

He leaned in and peered into her face as she closed the door behind them.

"What are you doing?' she asked, tucking in her chin like a disturbed turtle.

"Keekin' at yer face," he said, his gaze moving back and forth across her countenance as if he was using his eyes to paint her. "Does it ever keek different?"

She gaped at him. "Are you asking if my face can look *different?* What kind of thing is that to say? Is that a *request?*"

"Na. Ah had a dream and—" His voice faded. After a moment, he shook his head and walked toward the elevator without another word.

Catriona watched him go, one eye squinted, her lip curled with confusion.

"You are *so* weird," she muttered as the door clicked shut.

CHAPTER THREE

Catriona knew something was wrong the moment the elevator doors opened to the hotel lobby.

Thirty women grouped into a pulsating pod of bodies turned their eyes toward them at the same time, as if operating with a single mind.

Catriona expected people to gawk at Broch's kilt. Naturally, it inspired snickering in modern day America. But the way these women gaped—this was something different.

The pod drifted toward them, moving as a unit, a low murmur thrumming like an engine.

Catriona and Broch took two steps into the lobby before he stopped short and thrust his arm in front of her as if it were a railroad-crossing bar.

"Hold. Something isnae richt here," he said.

She cocked an eyebrow at him. "Yah think?"

"Aye."

She let it slide. He hadn't fully grasped modern day sarcasm.

Placing her hand on the arm he held in front of her, she pressed until he lowered it. "I think *you're* the one who needs to worry. They're staring at you, not me."

She didn't lie. All leers had locked on Broch and

the mob as a whole shifted to the right like a school of fish, gravitating toward him. The group drew tighter, creating a human shield between them and the exit.

Catriona took a step in front of Broch and held up her hands. "Ladies, is there—"

She cut short. Her step forward positioned her far enough into the lobby that she could see a banner hanging from the ceiling.

Welcome Knoxville Chapter of the Highlander Appreciation Clan (HAC).

Catriona turned her head, her eyes dropping to Broch's kilt.

Oh no.

As if on cue, the approaching group burst into frantic chatter.

"Will you sign my book?"

"Will you sign my chest?"

"It isn't him, it doesn't even look like him."

"Who cares?"

"Is he a stripper?"

"Oh I hope so."

The pleas and giggles grew louder. Catriona grabbed Broch's wrist.

"We've got to get out of here."

She pulled him forward, holding out her opposite arm to act as a pry bar, wedging them through the crowd.

"Are you wearing underwear under there?"

"Let's find out."

Broch made a strange whooping noise and Catriona glanced back in time to see a woman's hand sliding up his thigh. She slapped the woman's arm and received a scowl that could melt steel.

Broch looked at Catriona, his eyes wild. "Their hands are cold."

She'd seen Broch wrestle with armed men and never once did he look scared.

The ladies clearly terrified him.

The doors to outside opened and another group of women streamed into the hotel. Catriona saw a bus outside, ladies filing off it like ants on their way to a picnic.

Their progress toward escape slowed as more HAC members spotted Broch and orbited around him, as if he were a plaid sun and they, googly-eyed planets.

After a short argument with a woman who had shoved her aside, Catriona realized she'd lost Broch's hand. She spotted him, his head above the fray, floating away from her like a volleyball bobbing on the sea.

Soon, she could only hear his voice.

"Wummin'! Yer hands!"

The doors to a conference room opened on the far side of the lobby. Standing on her toes, Catriona spotted Broch, already on the stage in that room, defending the stairs to keep his admirers from climbing. The women filed out of the lobby and lined up in front of the stage, facing forward, as if awaiting Broch's command performance.

"Wummin', while ah appreciate yer attention, ye cannae be reachin' for my nether parts."

Giggles rippled through the room.

Then where are we supposed to put the dollar bills? called a voice from the back.

A group of women in the corner, not a single one a day younger than sixty, began chanting.

Take it off! Take it off!

Broch held up his hands. "Ah hae tae leave noo!"

"No!" screamed the women in unison.

Catriona pushed into the crowd.

"Ohmygawd listen to that accent," said a woman to her right.

"He might be better-looking than Jamie," said another.

"You shut your mouth with that blasphemy, or I will shut it for you," responded a third.

Catriona slipped away from the crowd and found her way into the room adjacent to the one in which Broch was still cornered. The door closed behind her and she leaned her back against it, taking a moment to appreciate the large, empty space. After all, it wasn't like Broch's *life* was in danger.

Probably.

The wall that separated her room from Broch's had a door. She opened it and found herself staring at a darkened backstage. On the opposite side of a large red curtain, she could hear Broch pleading with the ladies to allow him safe passage to the exit.

Catriona scurried to the curtain and pulled it far enough aside to peek onto the stage.

"Psst! Kilty!"

Broch's head whipped around as if he feared a

rear attack. His shoulders visibly relaxed upon seeing her.

"Git me oot o' here."

He bolted forward and she grabbed his hand to lead him through the darkened backstage. Feeling her way to the door, they escaped into the adjoining room. Behind them, jeers rose from the crowd.

Broch chuckled, seemingly giddy from the experience. "That was mad. Ah dinnae ken—"

Catriona stopped short and Broch bumped into the back of her. A woman stood between them and their escape route. From her frail frame, wrinkles and snowy white hair, Catriona guessed the lone-wolf to be at least eighty years-old. She wore a bright yellow sweatshirt with a picture of a shirtless Highlander and the phrase *Kilty Pleasures* scrawled beneath him in flamboyant script.

Catriona looked at Broch, who stared at the image on the sweatshirt, seemingly fascinated.

"Friend of yours?" she asked.

He looked at her, clearly confused.

"I just want to see the tummy," said the old woman.

Catriona's brow knit. "What?"

The woman nodded toward Broch. "I just want to see his tummy."

Catriona rubbed her eye with the palm of her hand. "Oh you've got to be kidding me."

"Whit does she want?" asked Broch.

"Lift your t-shirt and let's get out of here," muttered Catriona.

"Huh?"

"Just lift your tee. Let her see your six pack before the others figure out where we are, the way she did."

"Mah six pack?"

"Your *stomach*."

Still appearing unsure, Broch pulled up his t-shirt. The little old woman's eyes lit as if someone had found her on switch. She sucked in a breath as her hands fluttered to her mouth.

"Can I touch it?" she peeped.

"Oh come *on*," said Catriona.

"I'll scream," said the woman.

Catriona gaped. "*You'll* scream? You're the one trying to molest *him*."

The woman's jaw set. "I'll scream and let them *all* know he's in here."

"Look, lady—"

Broch touched Catriona's arm and took a step toward the woman.

The woman smiled. Lifting a shaking hand, she grazed his stomach with her fingertips before jerking back, giggling.

She stared up at him, beaming. "Thank you, young man."

"Yer fàilte," said Broch.

She chuckled. "Wait until I tell Betty. She is going to *die*." The woman pivoted and tottered toward the door.

"Dirty old lady," muttered Catriona.

Broch grinned. "Och. She's sweet. Ah think she fancied me."

Catriona sighed. "Let's go."

After employing some avoidance tactics that included wrapping Broch in a table cloth to hide his plaid, they escaped the hotel through the back entrance.

"That was insane," said Catriona when they were safe on the street.

"The more ah tried tae talk sense tae them, the more they ask me tae take aff mah clothes. Were they mad?"

"Something like that. But one thing is clear."

"Whit?"

"You can't stay in that hotel."

Finding no available cabs at the back exit and not daring to move to the front, Catriona retrieved her phone to call a car. As she worked her way through the taxi app, a nondescript black sedan pulled to the curb beside them. A familiar man stepped out, wincing as he did.

Catriona gasped.

"Sean, what are you doing here?" She rushed to her adopted father and helped him from the car. As expected, he waved her away and she had to wrestle him to assist.

"At least let me help you," she said, grunting.

"I'm fine."

She relented and took a step back, hands on her hips. "You should be in the hospital."

"I'm *fine*. They let me go," muttered Sean.

"Did they?"

"Yes."

"So if I call them, they won't tell me you went missing on them?"

Sean grimaced. "Uh—"

"That's what I thought."

Sean pointed to the hotel. "Go get your stuff. We're going home. I got ahold of Lulu and she diverted her plane from New York to here. Our ride arrives in three hours."

Lulu was Parasol Pictures studio's oldest living talent and its greatest diva. She also had the sex drive of a woman a quarter her age. The private plane she used to usher young studs all over the country had been their ride to Tennessee.

Catriona scowled.

"I shudder to think what you had to promise Lulu to arrange that."

"We have an understanding," said Sean.

Catriona thought about this for a moment. "Ew."

Sean rolled his eyes. "Oh stop. I'm way too old for her."

"You're twenty years younger."

"Exactly." He turned his attention to Broch, cocking his head to the side. "Is that a table cloth wrapped around you?"

"Aye. Tae hide me fae the mad wummin."

Sean looked at Catriona and she shook her head. "It's a long, strange story. I'll tell you on the plane."

Sean shrugged. "Go get your things."

Broch turned to re-enter the hotel and Catriona grabbed his arm.

"Oh no you don't. I'll get everything."

Sean scowled. "What's up?"

"Nothing. Stay out here with him. Don't let him talk to anyone and if you see a bunch of wild-eyed ladies heading for you, *run.*"

CHAPTER FOUR

1995 - Los Angeles, California

Rune didn't know how to explain how he knew he'd found the right place and time. Being in the wrong place was like having a second heartbeat perpetually out of synch with his own. When he arrived in 1995 California, the beats thumped in time.

That's when he knew he'd found her.

She was alive. He'd known it.

It took another six months to pinpoint the *exact* location of that second heartbeat, and when that happened, it happened by accident. He would never have recognized her if it hadn't been for a touch of serendipity.

Each day Rune awoke and began his search anew. His heart had pulled him to West Hollywood more than once, without success.

Still, he found himself there again.

After roaming the streets for hours, he abandoned his quest for the day and collapsed on a bench near a small children's park. On nearby benches, mothers read novels or engaged in chit-chat with one another, occasionally glancing from their pages to confirm their children's whereabouts and safety.

The mothers sometimes watched him, warily. Rune stared back until they turned away.

"I know you," said a voice.

Rune turned to find a child, no more than six years-old, staring at him. Dark hair cascaded around her freckled cheeks.

He scowled. "You *don't* know me. Go away."

The girl remained until he glanced her way once more.

"Yes, I do," she said.

He leaned forward, bending in half to bring his eyes to her level. "You don't—"

A shiver ran the length of his spine.

Those eyes.

He saw it in the child's eyes.

"Impossible," he whispered.

Giggling, the girl spun on her heel to return to her playmates.

He reached out. "Wait."

The girl stopped and blinked at him.

"Fiona?" he asked.

She wrinkled her nose. "You're weird."

"What's your name?"

She smiled and pulled at her dark hair. "Catriona."

Rune winced. His breath stopped short, as if someone had punched him in the solar plexus.

"Catty," called a woman's voice.

The girl snapped to attention. "Coming."

Catriona ran across the park to a dark-haired woman. The woman's glare locked on Rune, the corners of her mouth downturned. She pulled the girl into a protective embrace.

Rune looked away and rubbed his head with his hands.

"Something's wrong," he muttered, rocking in his seat. "No, no, no, no."

He looked back at the girl.

No. It's her. She's confused.

The young mother gathered her bags and, taking the girl's hand, headed toward the road. The girl skipped beside her mother to keep pace.

Fiona. I found you.

Rune stood and followed the woman at a safe distance. Her path led him several blocks away to a large house that had been converted into side-by-side residences. The woman lived on the right.

Staring at the building, Rune felt his heart strumming in time with the girl's. Euphoric, he returned to where he'd left his car and parked it a block away from the woman's townhouse.

He watched the home until long after night fell. No man came. No roommate. No one passed behind the large bay window but the woman and the child.

Time passed.

The second apartment to the left of the mother's was dark inside. No lights illuminated at nightfall. No one returned from work. Rune felt confident that the other half of the side-by-side was unoccupied.

It was almost as if this opportunity to be reunited with his daughter had been fated.

It was close to midnight when he made his move, springing to action like a shadow come to life. He strode across the street to the woman's door, its upper half segmented by panes of glass. Without hesitation, he put his fist through the pane closest to the knob and reached in to unlock the door.

By the time he entered the home, the woman was awake, standing in the hall like a statue. Stiff with fear.

He paused, staring at her. She wore a summer dress, her hair curled where, at the park, it had been straight and unkempt.

Why is she dressed?

She opened her mouth to scream and he bolted towards her, striking her in the stomach as he wrapped his arm around her neck. Breath forced from her lungs, she clawed at his arm as he dragged her toward her bedroom at the end of the hall.

Inside, he paused, holding her head tight against his body. She reached back to claw at his eyes, but he pulled back his neck, easily avoiding her.

Her struggling made it difficult to think.

Are there questions I should ask her? How did my daughter come to her? When?

She kicked him in the shin with her heel and he yelped. Grabbing her by the chest with his other arm, he gave her neck a sharp twist.

Her body fell limp, her full weight held aloft by his arm still clamped around her throat.

Rune dropped the body, the thud of her head sharp as it struck the hardwood floors.

So many questions unanswered.

Now I'll never know.

He wandered around the woman's apartment.

From what he could divine, her name was Cathy Foster and, gathering from the lack of photos in the house, she had no family. The only photo that he could find, other than a few snapshots of the dark-haired little girl, was hidden in her underwear drawer—a candid snapshot of the mother and a man he recognized, a B-actor by the name of Joe Wake.

Joe Wake was married to a washed-up actress. Rune couldn't recall her name. He'd seen things about them in the tabloids since arriving in Los Angeles. Perhaps that explained why Cathy was dressed and made-up at such a strange hour.

Late night rendezvous.

Shame on you, Cathy Foster.

It sickened him that his daughter had been in the possession of such a harlot.

He threw the photo at the woman's body and it fluttered down to rest beside her.

Rune didn't like that a man with money and influence might miss Cathy Foster, but Joe Wake was tangled in an illicit affair—there was little chance he'd make trouble.

Nothing left to learn, Rune entered the only remaining room.

Inside, the girl lay sleeping, her arms wrapped around a stuffed pink bear.

He walked to the bed and lifted her into his arms.

"Who are you?" she mumbled, eyes still closed as she rubbed at them.

"I'm your mommy's friend."

"Where's Mommy?"

"I'm taking you to her. She had to go out and asked me to come get you."

The girl pushed off his chest and peered into his face.

"I know you," she said.

He smiled. "I know you, too."

He walked her to his car. As he finished buckling her into his back seat, a red Ferrari pulled across from Cathy's house and parked.

Rune straightened, staring at it.

A man stepped out of the Ferrari and his attention swiveled towards Rune.

It was dark. Rune didn't think the man could see him.

But still.

CHAPTER FIVE

Back home in Hollywood, Catriona lay on her sofa, staring at the ceiling.

She glanced at the clock on her oven. *Five p.m.* She needed to get dressed for dinner. Sean had asked Brochan and her to join him, and he'd promised to shed light on the recent oddities in their lives. After nearly a week of her begging him for answers, he'd finally relented.

It felt good to be back in her apartment above Parasol Picture's employment office. She'd missed glancing out her window to find a fifteen-foot dragon's head rolling by, or a man dressed like a three-eyed alien.

Those apartment ads that touted *room with a view* had no idea how interesting a view could get.

Stretching, Catriona stood and moved to her tiny en suite bathroom. She turned the shower knobs to her regular positions and undressed. Eager to relax beneath a hot shower, she stepped in, and with a shriek, scrambled back out.

The water was *chilly*. Not cold, but certainly not the steamy shower she'd hoped to enjoy. She turned the hot knob as far as it would go to experience little change in temperature.

Cursing under her breath, she cut the water and stood staring at the knobs, as if they'd confess their sins under pressure. She'd never had problems with the hot water before and wasn't sure what to do.

Slipping into her robe, she wandered into the kitchen to test the sink there.

No hot water.

She stared at the wall separating her from Broch's apartment, chewing the inside of her cheek, deep in thought.

That would be a good place to start. First, she'd test Broch's shower to find out if it was only her apartment with no hot water, or if the whole building had run out. Then, at least she'd have something intelligent to share with maintenance before she called.

She huffed. How handy that Sean had *immediately* given Broch the apartment right next door to the apartment she'd *begged* to use for years.

Exiting her apartment, she walked down the hall to knock on Brochan's door.

No one answered.

She sighed, certain that he was inside, and tried again.

"I know you're in there," she called.

Nothing.

She bobbed her head back and forth weighing the pros and cons of unlocking the door with her master key. *What's the worst that could happen?* It wasn't as though she hadn't seen him naked before. The man tore off his clothes at every opportunity, like a strong-willed two-year-old.

Jogging back to her apartment, Catriona grabbed her keys and returned to unlock his door.

She poked her head inside.

"Broch?"

The room appeared to be filled with smoke.

Oh no. She'd been meaning to show him how to use modern appliances before he burned down the building, and now it was too late.

"Broch!"

She plunged into the room.

"Broch!"

The Highlander remained missing, but she could see nothing was on his stove. Most of the smoke gathered at the entrance to the bedroom.

With Broch and his eighteenth century proclivities, it was impossible to guess what she might find. Her first thought was that he'd been chilly and built a fire in his room to keep warm.

She strode to the bedroom, where it proved even harder to see. Only then did it occur to her that the smoke had no smell.

Not only that, it felt *wet.*

It wasn't smoke at all.

It was steam.

She heard the hiss of the shower. The mist was so thick, it looked as though Broch had spent the last hour filming *Hounds of the Baskervilles* in his bedroom.

"Broch!"

"Eh?" came a call from inside the bathroom.

"What are you doing?"

"Ah'm bathin'. This water gits sae *het.* Tis lik

heaven."

She raised her arms in agitation, though she knew the chances that he could see her were slim. "No wonder I can't get any hot water. You've used it all. It looks like the moors at midnight out here."

"It runs oot?"

"Yes, it runs *oot.*"

"I wis just thinkin' t'wasn't as warm as t'was, but now it feels more lik' whit ah'm used tae, which is nice, tae."

She threw back her head and let out a grunt of frustration. "Get out and get dressed for dinner, you big goof. I'm going to go suffer through a lukewarm shower."

"Aye. Ah will. Ah'm coolin' myself."

She stormed back to her apartment and prepared for their meeting with Sean. After the fastest shower ever taken, she was still muttering under her breath as she slipped into a dress she hadn't worn for nearly a year. Sean had said to wear something *nice.*

As a rule, her work called for *stain-proof* more often than *nice*, so it felt good to get gussied-up.

By the time she put on her makeup, her ire over Broch's water use had faded. She was too excited to stay mad any longer.

She was nervous to hear what Sean would share with them. She took heart that the fancy evening had all the earmarks of a celebratory dinner.

That has to bode well, doesn't it?

Make-upped and heeled, she returned to the hallway to knock on Broch's door. This time, the door flung open and Broch stood before her in a t-shirt and a kilt.

Not again.

He grinned. "Keek at *ye*. How come yer sae tall?"

She crossed her right leg in front of her left shin so he could see her heels.

His expression said he was impressed. "Och. 'Tis quite a shank ye hae there."

She scowled and dropped her leg.

"That's a bonnie dress yer wearin'. And yer locks are sae—" He reached out and fluffed her hair.

"Hey!" Scowling, she stepped back, arranging her locks back into place. She pointed at his shirt. On it, a penguin wearing a top hat rested a flipper on a fancy walking cane.

"Where do you even find these shirts?" she asked.

He pulled the tee out from his body and peered down at it. "It's a bird in a bunnet," he said, chuckling.

"I see that. Sean said to wear something *nice*."

"Aye. He's wearing a bow on his neck. See?" He pointed to the penguin's bow tie.

"So that makes it your formal tee shirt?"

"Aye. He has a walkin' cane as well."

"I think Sean was thinking something a little more formal for *you*, not the bird."

Broch thought for a moment and then nodded. "Oh. Aye." He flipped up the gathering of fabric at the back of his kilt and crossed it across his chest, securing it with a simple round brooch he'd had pinned to the waistband. "There. Ready?"

She made a mental note to ask costuming for an

intervention with him.

"Perfect." She walked past him to the elevator, pushed the call button and stood waiting for him to join her. As he did, she mumbled. "I hope you're at least wearing the underwear I bought you."

His eyes lit. "Aye. Ah love thaim." He lifted his kilt and she saw he wore the boxer briefs she'd bought for him upon their return to Hollywood, his muscular thighs bulging from the bottom of them. She caught the outline of what else the briefs packaged and looked away, her cheeks feeling flush.

He grinned. "They're lik' a wee hug, doon below."

She took a deep breath as the doors opened. "Baby steps."

He followed, still beaming as he dropped his kilt.

She caught him looking at her sidelong, a smirk on his face.

She turned to him. "You're doing all this on purpose to drive me crazy, aren't you?"

"Whit?"

"You know exactly what you're doing. You like to watch me squirm."

He shook his head. "Ah dinnae ken whit ye mean."

Turning forward, he pressed his lips together as if to keep from laughing. After a moment he tilted sideways toward her, without looking at her.

"Ye keek beautiful," he mumbled.

She turned away to hide her smile.

CHAPTER SIX

1995 – Los Angeles, California

Joe Wake paused, his hand resting on the knob of his back door.

Something felt off, as if a furry little spider leg was scratching at the back of his neck. Tapping.

SOS. SOS.

Something was *wrong*. He could feel it.

He turned and walked back through his living room, the only illumination provided by the tiny spotlight forever trained on his Emmy award. It wasn't vanity that kept the light on. The switch that controlled that beam ran independently from the room's other switches and was a pain to turn off, so it remained on, serving as a makeshift nightlight for midnight snacking.

Joe re-entered his bedroom, closed the en suite bathroom door but for a crack, and turned on the bathroom's light.

His wife Theresa's face was turned away from the light. His wife slept hard. She drank. Still, she'd awoken before, nearly catching him sneaking out to visit his girlfriend.

He'd shared the story of his near-capture with his

girlfriend, Cathy. Cathy's friend was with them at the time, and the girl told him that she used to crush a sleeping pill in her ex-boyfriend's drink each night. She said he had a tendency to wake up in the middle of the night, half drunk and half hungover, mad at the world. So she made sure he *didn't* wake up and slept better herself.

He'd tried the trick on Theresa and it worked better than he could have imagined. He could dress, leave the house to spend a few hours with Cathy, come back, undress, and Theresa would barely move a muscle throughout. In the morning, she'd wake up refreshed and none the wiser.

But now...

Something isn't right.

He moved toward the bed and lowered his hand to Theresa's ribs.

He felt no movement.

Reluctant to wake her for fear he'd miss his date, he retracted his hand and stared at his wife for a minute.

She's breathing, right?

No one died from one sleeping pill. Did they?

That's when he smelled it. A pungent citrus scent. It was a little like his wife's breath after she had grapefruit and vodkas.

Bending at the waist, he sniffed his wife. Near her face the smell was the strongest, but her head blocked the light leaking from the bathroom and he couldn't see much.

Placing a single finger on her shoulder, he pulled

her onto her back, his teeth locked in a grimace of expectation. She was going to wake up and scream.

She didn't.

Theresa's mouth gaped, her skin pale in the glow of the bathroom light. Chunks of tan mush clung to her lips and cheek. Her eyes were open. Unmoving. Unblinking.

He swallowed as he processed this new data. Then, something in his mind snapped free and he sprang into action.

"Theresa!" He shook her, her body bouncing on the bed without resistance. He touched her face and found it cold.

He gasped and stepped back.

Dead.

Already, the tabloid headlines swirled in his skull.

He'd never work again.

Hell, he'd never see the light of day again.

He'd be thrown into jail to rot.

He stared down at his wife and felt a pang of remorse. There was the *loss* of Theresa to contend with as well. She was lazy, demanding, a bit of a nightmare but, he did love her in his way. She was like a pair of old shoes that caused blisters, but at one time, they'd been his favorite pair of shoes—

He flopped into a stuffed chair.

What am I thinking? I just killed my wife and I'm standing here comparing her to a pair of loafers.

He stared at the arm of the chair, tracing the flowers on it with a fingertip.

I hate this pattern.

He could get rid of the chair now. Claim the rest of the closet. Get rid of the pink wallpaper in the spare bathroom—

Stop it.

This wasn't a chance to redecorate. It was a nightmare. These days, DNA and other crime testing was so sophisticated they'd certainly find the sleeping medicine in her body.

Fingerprints.

He turned to the bathroom where the light still glowed, as if nothing had happened. As if it hadn't shown him his dead wife.

The pill bottle.

He stood and flung open his closet, retrieving the bottle of sleeping pills he kept hidden in an old loafer.

He chuckled, recalling his earlier thoughts.

I hid the pills in an old loafer. How ironic.

Grabbing a sock, he rubbed down the bottle to remove any fingerprints.

No.

That would be weird if they found a bottle with *no* finger prints. He left the walk-in and approached the body of his wife, her frozen stare still gawking at the ceiling, her face speckled with chicken piccata. Gingerly lifting her hand, he pressed her fingers against the bottle and then, with his hand in the sock like a puppet, he carried the bottle to the bathroom and put it in the medicine cabinet.

What now? Crawl in bed and pretend to find her in the morning?

He shivered at the thought of it.

Reaching for his phone he dialed his girlfriend.

Cathy will know what to do. She was a nurse—

He stopped one digit short of completion.

No. It's too late for CPR.

He looked at his wife. Was it too late? Had he missed an opportunity?

Leaning in with the idea of attempting mouth-to-mouth, he spotted a speck of the evening's spinach salad hanging from his wife's lip and gagged.

No. Too late for CPR. Definitely.

He took a second to allow his roiling stomach to settle and tried dialing again. Cathy couldn't raise the dead; but, he had to at least *warn* her. She had to know it was more important than *ever* that their affair remain a secret. And, he had to ensure that her friend, if questioned, wouldn't tell the cops that Theresa died the same way she'd told him she'd knocked out her boyfriend.

That would be bad.

He dialed six numbers and then stopped.

Phone records. He couldn't call Cathy. He needed to see her in person.

Joe grabbed his keys, bolted to his car and sped to Cathy's house in West Hollywood. In his head, he ran through all the possible ways he could explain to her what had happened. He had to spin every sentence to ensure she pictured Theresa's death as a terrible *accident.* That his wife overdosed.

Yes. She overdosed on sleeping pills.

He knew Theresa as such a sound sleeper that the obvious answer to his problems hadn't even occurred to him. He'd tell Cathy that Theresa had been having trouble sleeping. *Thank god I never told her I'd been using the sleeping pills to safely sneak in and out of the house.*

He'd been too ashamed to tell his girlfriend the great lengths to which he'd gone to cheat on Theresa. If Cathy knew how terrified he was of his wife, she'd be disgusted. Plus, he'd found it best to never hand girlfriends extra ammunition. Break-ups happened—some ran more smoothly than others.

Arriving at Cathy's apartment, he leapt out of the Ferrari and immediately heard another car door slam. He flinched and turned toward the noise. A block away, a man stood next to a car. His head was turned in Joe's direction.

Crap.

He spun away and pretended to walk down the street, glancing over his shoulder until he saw the man drive away.

Whew.

He boomeranged back to Cathy's apartment.

Joe found Cathy's front door cracked open. Though it was possible she'd left it open for their evening rendezvous, it seemed odd. As a single woman with a small child, Cathy always erred on the side of safety.

For the second time that evening, he knew something was not right. His mouth went dry as he pushed open the door.

His first step into the house made a crunching sound. He felt something grind beneath his shoe. By the dull glow of the outside street light, he saw glass glittering on the ground inside the door.

That's when he noticed the broken pane.

His blood ran cold.

I left the scene of one crime to enter the scene of another.

"Cathy?" he called, the word sticking in his throat. He coughed and tried again.

"Cathy?"

Tip-toeing toward the back of the house, he paused to peer into the child's room.

Empty.

He chewed his tongue in an attempt to work up some saliva.

"Cathy?" he called again.

No response.

He flicked a switch on the wall and the hall light buzzed to life. The soft glow made him feel a little better. In the movies, intruders always cut the lines. If the lights worked, that was a good sign.

He closed his eyes and daydreamed about a time he and Cathy would laugh about this evening.

Something had broken the window and the frightened girl went to sleep in her mother's bed. That's all. Nothing sinister.

Continuing down the hall, he entered his girlfriend's bedroom.

Cathy's body lay on the ground beside her bed, her eyes open, glistening in the light from the hall. He saw no blood or wounds, but her neck twisted at an unnatural angle.

Joe collapsed to his knees.

His wife and girlfriend both dead on the same

evening.

There was a square of paper beside Cathy.

He picked it up and turned it over.

In the dim light he could see it was a photo of Cathy and him.

Together.

He blanched, and his mind cleared but for a single, urgent thought.

I have to get back home.

If there was a possibility that people would suspect that he had something to do with *Cathy's* death, he'd never convince anyone he was guilt-free of *Theresa's.*

He stuffed the photo in his pocket. Removing his sock, he wiped everything he'd touched and bolted back to his Ferrari.

Trembling, he found it impossible to insert his key in the ignition. He took a deep breath and used his opposite hand to steady the first. The key entered the hole. With a twist, the engine roared to life. He made a mental note to sell the old sports car and get something more likely to inspire sympathy.

Widowers in sports cars were always guilty of something.

He gasped at the sound of the word in his head.

Widower.

I'm a widower.

He perked, mood lightening. *Girls love widowers.*

Ashamed, he shook his head like a wet dog in an attempt to rid himself of evil thoughts.

Stop it. Drive.

Not far from home, it occurred to him that *anyone* could have seen him driving. Any story of sleeping all night beside his dead wife would be blown.

He stopped at a gas station and found a payphone. He called Parasol Picture's emergency line, the line he was never to call except in situations of life and death. This counted. Twice.

When he finished conveying his vague need for help, he walked into the gas station and searched for an item that a person might run out in the middle of the night to buy. He settled on toothpaste.

At home he hid the toothpaste already in his bathroom and pushed Theresa back on her side. She'd begun to stiffen and he had to force her arm back into a more natural position.

When he felt she looked most natural, he stood, fists clenched, willing himself to stay calm until the studio's fixers arrived.

He made it forty-five seconds before the phone rang. Startled, he yipped.

Grabbing his chest with one hand he braced himself for the next ring, praying it never came.

It did.

He took a deep breath and answered the phone. "Hello?"

"Did you kill your girlfriend?"

Joe's breathing stopped. "What?"

"Did you kill Cathy Foster?"

At the sound of Cathy's name, he slapped a hand over his mouth to keep from screaming. He moved a finger to answer. "Who is this?"

"I know who killed her. But it *looks* like you did."

"Oh god..."

"56 Grapevine Drive. Now."

The phone clicked.

Joe remained with the receiver at his ear, unable to move for several minutes. Finally, he set it down and, heading back into his closet, retrieved a small vial of cocaine.

He snorted all that remained and, feeling stronger, once again ran to find his car keys.

Half-way to the Ferrari he turned and ran back into the house to get his gun.

CHAPTER SEVEN

1995 – Los Angeles, California

Sean's gaze swept across the darkened Parasol Pictures studio lot. He preferred the lot at night, without the bustle of movie production thrumming at every turn. His new Motorola Startac clamshell phone rang and he jumped.

I'll never get used to these damn things.

The bigwigs at the studio had insisted he carry a cell phone, but he hated it. Allowing people to reach him at any time or place was a torture he couldn't have imagined. Before cell phones, people had time to reconsider how important their needs were. In the time it took to find a landline and call him for help, people often changed their minds or handled their own business. Now, as soon as the tiniest thing went wrong, an actor was on his or her ever-present cell phone, begging him to come running.

Groaning, he opened the phone.

"Hello?"

The voice of studio Vice President Dom Gastaldi boomed on the opposite end of the connection. Sean jerked the phone from his ear to keep from being deafened.

"Sean, I need you to find Joe Wake. He called the emergency line. Something about his wife."

Sean recognized the name of one of the studio's most prolific B-actors. Joe was a mealy-mouthed little man who'd made a career out of playing cuckolded husbands and cowering shopkeepers held at gunpoint by thieves.

"Did Theresa finally kill him?"

"The opposite, if anything."

"What? What happened?"

"Who knows? All I know is that he's got a shoot on Wednesday. We had the kangaroos shipped here special and it would cost a fortune to reschedule the scene. I need you to find him and sort this all out before the cops do their usual bang-up job."

"Or before he hurts himself or someone else."

"Sure. Whatever."

"Did you call Luther?"

"I called *you*."

"Any idea where to start?"

"I think Joe's home. Let me know when you have him."

Dom disconnected.

Sean clapped shut his phone. He *did* find the crisp *snap!* of ending a call on the accursed thing strangely satisfying.

Walking towards his car, he opened the phone again to call his partner, Luther. As small as Joe Wake was, it never hurt to bring back-up to an unknown situation.

Big Luther was more than back-up—he was a

howitzer.

Sean arrived at Luther's to find his friend standing on the sidewalk, waiting. Luther was six-foot-six of pure muscle. Three tours in Vietnam had made him as tough as he was strong. Sean knew that deep in that over-sized chest beat a puppy-dog's heart, but that was a side of Luther few ever saw.

Luther had no time for fools. Sadly, *fools* made up ninety percent of their clients.

Luther folded himself into Sean's Jaguar and they headed for Laurel Canyon.

"Did I wake you?" asked Sean.

"You know you didn't."

"Did you hear anything about Joe?"

"Just what you told me—that Joe and his wife are into it." Luther pulled a pack of cigarettes from his jacket, dragged one out and rolled it back and forth in his fingers. "She probably beat the crap out of him."

"Dom told me, from what he can tell, it's the opposite."

Luther laughed. "I don't believe that for a second."

"I don't either." Sean chuckled and glanced at his friend, nodding toward his cigarette. "Those things are going to kill *you*."

"Lotta things linin' up to kill me. No particular order."

"They're going to make my car stink, too. You know the rules."

Luther huffed and slid the cigarette back into his pack. "You and this car. It ain't healthy."

"Right. And smoking is?"

Luther turned his attention outside. "Where we goin'? The Canyon?"

"Yep. Dom thinks he's home. We'll start there and see where it leads us."

On Laurel Canyon Boulevard, a pair of lights approached them, closing rapidly. A red Ferrari roared past them. They looked at each other to confirm their suspicions.

"That's him," they said in tandem.

Sean cursed under his breath. "Where's he going like that? This isn't like him."

The car had been an odd choice for Joe, and Sean had joked with Luther that the actor had hit his mid-life crisis. Perhaps he'd been more right than he suspected.

Sean arced into a U-turn and Luther braced himself to keep from being thrown against the door. Sean punched the gas.

"You're never gonna catch him in that crazy Italian car of his," said Luther.

The rearview lights they'd been following turned into a neighborhood.

"Doesn't look like I'm going to have to."

They reached the spot where the Ferrari had turned and found it led to a cluster of Spanish-style row-mansions. Joe Wake peeled into a driveway, bottoming out his sports car with the horrific sound of metal on cement.

Sean screeched his Jaguar to a stop at the curb. Joe was already at the door of a home, pounding with one hand and waving what looked like a gun in the other.

"Does that look like a gun to you?" asked Sean.

Luther nodded. "What the hell is going on with that little man?"

Sean leaned over Luther and pulled his own gun from the glove compartment before jumping out of the car. Luther stepped from his side and walked around to join Sean. Using the car as a barrier between themselves and Joe, they watched the actor scream at the door, demanding to be let inside.

"Joe!" called Sean.

At the sound of Sean's voice, Joe turned and lowered his gun, his mouth gaping with surprise.

"Sean? How did you find me here?"

"Joe, put down—"

Joe interrupted. "Sean, you have to help me. There's someone trying to blackmail me."

Behind Joe, the home's large brown door cracked open. A hand reached out and slapped hard on Joe's shoulder, jerking him inside with such force it appeared as if the diminutive actor had been lifted off his feet.

The door slammed shut and the night fell silent again, as if Joe had never been there.

"What just happened?" asked Sean.

"Nothin' good," said Luther.

Sean moved from behind the car and headed towards the house. Luther fell in behind him.

"Any idea whose place this is?" asked Sean.

"Nope."

At the front door, they paused on the landing. Luther retrieved the gun he wore tucked in his shoulder holster, hidden beneath a flannel shirt big enough to serve as a horse blanket.

Sean tried the door. The knob turned easily. He opened the door a crack.

"Joe?"

The house remained silent.

He called again. "Joe, it's Sean and Luther. We're here to help. Why don't you come on out?"

They heard Joe scream out. "No! I'll kill you, you son of a—" His outburst ceased as abruptly as it had begun.

Sean motioned for Luther to get behind him as they entered the home. Sean's Glock 21 led the way, pointed out and down.

Upon reaching the first archway Sean paused, back against the wall, and peeked around the corner.

Joe stood in the center of a large living room. He held his gun pointed at someone on the opposite side of the room and out of sight. His hands shook.

"Joe, we're here. Put down the gun."

Joe glanced at Sean. He sniffed, his eyes wild, jaw working side to side.

"What's up?" Luther whispered.

Sean grunted. "He's coked out of his mind and holding a gun on someone, but I can't see who. Get to the other side, I'll keep him occupied."

Sean again peered around the corner and motioned to his partner that it was safe to move. Luther dashed to the opposite side of the archway, he and Sean taking sentry positions on either side of the arch.

"I saw that!" screamed Joe, his voice echoing in the cathedral-ceilinged living room.

"Joe, this isn't you. Put down the gun," said Sean in his most soothing tone.

Joe swung the gun in Sean's direction and Sean ducked back behind the wall.

"Sean, this man's lying. I think he tried to kill me, I swear. He's—"

There was a yip, followed by scuffling and a succession of thumps. Sean dropped to his knees and slid into the archway, gun drawn.

A tall, thin man stood where Joe had been. His features were sharp, his disheveled gray hair spilling in greasy clumps across his forehead. Joe lay crumpled at his feet, blood streaming from his nose.

Sean kept his gun trained on the man. "Take it easy, buddy."

Without answering, the man bent down and plucked Joe's gun from his hand.

Sean rose to his feet. "We're here to *help*. It might not look like it, what with me holding a gun on you, but you're making me nervous. I apologize for whatever Joe's done, but right now I need you to drop that gun."

The man straightened, the gun at his side. His arm lifted and, without taking his eyes off Sean, he shot Joe Wake in the head.

CHAPTER EIGHT

1995 – Los Angeles, California

With Joe Wake on the ground with a single hole in his skull, the gaunt stranger swung his gun at Sean and fired again.

Sean spun away behind the wall separating the living room and foyer. He took a quick personal inventory.

Not hit.

It became clear *why* he'd remained unharmed.

The bullet wasn't intended for him.

Luther stumbled back and struck the iron railings of a staircase before sliding to a sitting position. From his angle, Sean could see blood staining Luther's t-shirt beneath his flannel. Judging from the sound of airy wheezing, Sean guessed the bullet had perforated his friend's lung.

Sean peeked into the living room, only to feel a hand clamp on his wrist.

The man had been standing directly behind the wall, waiting.

Jerking him into the room and pulling the gun from his hand in one swift motion, the man sent Sean's Glock skittering down the hallway behind them. As his attacker raised his own weapon, Sean chopped at his arm and watched as the gun tumbled toward Luther. It slid on the tile until it stopped near his injured partner's foot, revolving like the world's worst game of spin the bottle.

Luther remained still, his expression slack. He stared at the stranger from beneath heavy lids, as if daring him to make a play for the gun.

The gaunt man pushed Sean, who tripped over Joe Wake's leg and fell into a side table, splintering it into kindling as he fell.

As he scrambled to regain his feet, Sean heard the sound of scraping metal. He looked up in time to see his foe yank a sword from where it had been mounted on the wall and raise the weapon above his head.

Sean rolled away as the blade fell. He could feel the air move at the back of his neck and hear the heft of the ancient weapon as it hit the floor. It sunk into the floor boards and stuck fast.

Sean scrambled past the man on his hands and knees. A second sword remained above the fireplace and Sean leapt to jerk it from the wall. It released in time for him to block his enemy's blade as it swept at him at waist level.

Pushing away from the attack, Sean backed toward the front window and held the sword aloft. It felt strange, yet comfortable in his hands. It had been a long time since he'd wielded such a blade.

The men squared off on either side of a low glass coffee table.

"You don't know how to use that," said the dark-haired man.

Sean smiled. "I think you'll find I do."

The man stepped around the table and thrust forward. Sean parried and, pushing off the sofa with one foot, assumed his enemy's original position.

The man's eyes narrowed. "Who are you?"

Sean remained silent, concentrating. He couldn't allow the battle to continue. He needed to get Luther to a hospital.

Sean took a step back, nearly tripping again over the lifeless body of Joe Wake. He saw a flash of movement at the end of the hall that presumably led to the bedrooms, and readied his sword, preparing to skewer this new approaching attacker.

A raven-haired little girl walked to the end of the hall and stared up at Sean. She held a gun in her tiny hands.

Sean recognized the weapon as his own, the one the man had tossed down the hall.

He glanced at his adversary. The man's eyes grew wide and he pointed at the girl.

"Don't touch her."

Sean scooped the girl into the crook of his left arm. She dropped the gun to the tile floor and wrapped her arms around his neck.

Roaring, the gaunt man kicked the table between them, shattering the glass and flipping the flimsy frame onto the sofa as he cleared a path for his attack.

He thrust forward with his weapon and Sean raised his own, praying that his right arm would be strong enough to reject the blow. Twisting his body to protect the girl from the blade, he felt her jump as the crack of gunfire echoed.

The dark man's blade jerked to the right, his legs buckling beneath him. Seeing his opportunity, Sean swung, catching the man at the shoulder, slicing deep into his upper chest with the heavy broadsword.

The man folded back, his sword clattering to the ground.

Sean turned toward the source of the gun blast to find Luther had crawled from the foyer. He lay on the ground, gun in his hand, breathing as if through a clogged snorkel.

"It's about time," said Sean.

"Screw you," said Luther.

The man on the ground moaned. A pool of blood had collected around the fallen swordsman and Sean pressed the girl's head against his chest to keep her from seeing.

"Who are you?" asked Sean.

The man ignored him, his stare locking on the girl.

"I'll return for you," he whispered.

A bright flash of light exploded from where the man lay and Sean reeled back, covering his eyes. When he could focus again, the man was gone.

"Where'd he go?" asked Luther between labored breaths.

His arm tiring, Sean appraised the room. There seemed to be no appropriate place to place a child. He wanted to remove her from the mayhem. Already, she'd stepped over a dead body to watch him split a man in two with a sword. The therapy bills were piling up.

Dropping his weapon with a clatter, he walked the girl into the foyer and set her down.

"You stay here," he said.

She nodded, her dark blue eyes unreadable as a Scottish loch. He patted the girl on the arm and moved back to the living room to check on Luther.

"How you doing?"

Luther squinted at him and took a watery breath. "Never better. You?"

Sean pulled out his phone. "It's a great Darth Vader imitation you have there, if that's any consolation."

"When this is over, I'm going to kick your ass."

Sean grinned, squatted on his heels and put pressure on Luther's wound. The big man winced.

"Put your hand there. I have to make a call," said Sean.

"It hurts."

"Stop being a baby and do it."

Luther put his hand on his wound.

"I need you to do me a favor," said Sean.

Luther looked at him. "Sure, anything. I've got nothin' else to do."

"Don't say a word about the girl."

Luther cocked his head. "The little girl?"

Sean nodded. "I need to take her. She was never here."

"Are you kidding?"

"It's important. I'll explain it all later." Sean dialed 911.

"What about the man?" Luther did his best to prop himself against the wall. The expression on his friend's face told Sean that every movement was a lesson in agony.

Sean spoke to the emergency operator and, ignoring instructions to stay on the line, snapped shut his phone. He looked where the dark man had last lain. Even the blood pooling beneath his attacker had disappeared.

"Don't mention him. He wasn't here either. Or, he was—but he ran out after shooting Joe and you."

"So you were never here either, I suppose?"

Sean shook his head. "No. Tell the cops you came in to find Joe dead. You struggled with the guy, he shot you and then ran away—" Sean paused, realizing how crazy the story already sounded. "Better yet—act like you can't talk and I'll come figure out the story with you in the hospital."

Luther slumped, his expression pinched, muttering. "Leavin' a black man with a dead white man. I don't like this one bit. Give me your phone."

Already turning to leave, Sean stopped. "What?"

"You made the 911 with your phone."

"Shite. Good point."

Sean patted him on the shoulder and placed the phone beside his friend before returning to the girl. He knelt beside her.

"We need to go now," he said, lifting her.

"Will you take me to my mother?"

Sean grimaced. "Sure. We can talk about that."

She clung to his neck as he opened the door and

strode quickly down the house path to the sidewalk. "Mommy can't find me because he changed my name," said the girl as he reached the end of the block and turned. In the distance, he could hear sirens.

"The man changed your name?"

"Yes."

"What's your real name?"

"My name is Catriona."

"Ah, that's a pretty name for a brave girl. That's what I'll call you, okay?"

The girl smiled and hugged his neck.

CHAPTER NINE

"You're breaking up with me," said Catriona.

Sean scowled. "What?"

Catriona looked around the restaurant. Sean had *never* taken her to a place as fancy as the one where they now sat. When he told her he was ready to share his past and explain the cryptic comment he'd made in the hospital about her possible time-traveling abilities, she'd thought his choice of venue meant the story would be worth celebrating. It wasn't until she sat down that she realized she'd read it all wrong.

She was surrounded by strangers enjoying their expensive meals, none of whom could ever dream that the men at a nearby table had traveled from the eighteenth century.

And one of these men has tricked me.

"You brought me here so I couldn't scream at you," she said, glowering at Sean.

He grimaced, confirming her suspicion.

Catriona smacked the table top with the tip of her fingers. "I *knew* it. You're trying to keep me from making a scene."

The occupants of several nearby tables turned to look at her.

"If his plan is tae keep ye quiet, it isnae workin',"

said Broch.

Catriona flashed the other diners an apologetic smile and stared at her napkin. *This can't be a good sign.* Sean didn't trust her to take the revelation of his and Broch's secrets like an adult. The news was *that* bad.

While her emotions ping-ponged inside of her breast, Broch sat between them, calm and happy. Though he was the visitor, *she* felt like the third wheel.

"Would you like some bread?" said a waiter, arriving with a basket in his hand.

"Aye, ah'm starving, taa." Brochan took the basket from the man's hand and set it down in front of him. He nodded to the others. "They'd lik' some tae, aye?"

The waiter stared down at him before turning to Catriona and Sean. "Would, uh, you *each* like a basket of bread?"

Catriona closed her eyes and shook her head. "We're fine, thank you."

Broch glanced at her, chewing. "Are ye sure? The breid 'tis delicious. Ah think there's a wee bit of honey in it."

Catriona turned her attention back to Sean, nodding her head towards Broch. "Just so you know, I *believe* that he's from eighteenth-century Scotland. I wasn't sure at first, what with his sophisticated manners and all, but I made the leap."

Broch stopped chewing and stared at her.

"Ah ken Sassenach, lassie."

"You know sasquatch?" Catriona looked at Sean.

"Is *that* what you brought me here to tell me?"

Sean rolled his eyes. "He said he speaks English."

"Oh sure. That totally sounded like English."

"He means he knows when you're mocking him." Sean nodded to Broch's personal basket and leaned in to speak in a whisper. "The waiter is supposed to give you *one* piece of bread from the basket. It wasn't all for you."

Broch shot Catriona a look. "Howfur am ah suppose tae ken whit breid is mines if ye dinnae tell me?"

He pushed the basket into the middle of the table and sat back, arms folded across his chest, his lips drawn into a knot.

"He's got a point. You can't set him up to fail," said Sean.

Catriona sighed. Sean was taking Broch's side.

She put her hands on the table and leaned forward to lock gazes with Sean. "Fine. *Sorry*. Now spit out your whole sordid story. The one you should have told me a long time ago. I promise not to make a scene."

"Ah wouldnae believe her," mumbled Broch.

Sean seemed to brace himself to speak. "Sweetheart—"

"Don't *sweetheart* me," said Catriona.

Broch pointed at Catriona. "Ha. See? Ah tellt ye. She's angry as a cat in a loch."

Sean flashed Broch a warning look and began again. "Cat, do you remember anything about the day I found you?"

Catriona sat back in her chair and shook her head.

"Not a lot. You've always told me that I was adopted and I think I created the memory of living in an orphanage out of scenes from *Annie*. But now...I think I have a memory of you cutting off a man's arm with a sword? I didn't think it was a real memory until recently, when it came to my attention that catching you sword fighting maybe wasn't as odd as I once thought."

Sean perked. "Right. That's *right*. The man you were with shot a client of mine and Luther."

"I can't picture what happened after you hit him with the sword..." She waggled a finger from him to Broch and back again. "Am I right to assume he was a time-traveler like you two? Did he jump through time after being injured?"

"Yes. He was in a bad way when he jumped—but he might have found help on the other side—"

"Where did ye pat yer cloth?" said a loud whisper in Catriona's ear. Broch had leaned towards her, holding his napkin wadded in his hand.

She glared at him. "It goes in your lap."

He winked. "Aye. Ah thought as much. Ta."

"Do you *mind*? We're trying to have a serious conversation here."

"Aye, sorry."

Broch leaned back and, catching a stare from a woman at a nearby table, smiled and tipped an invisible cap to her. She giggled and turned away.

Catriona returned her attention to Sean. "So that's why you kept me? Why you hid me from the police? Because the man who had me was one of you?"

He nodded.

"Who was that man?"

"I don't know."

"And if he lived—does that mean he'll come looking for me again?"

"It's possible."

Catriona swallowed, frightened to ask her next question. "Do you think he was my father?"

Sean released a breath, his shoulders falling. "I don't know. But, it's certainly possible."

"You're full of information."

"That's half the reason I never talked to you about this before. I don't know much."

"So if that man jumped through time after you wounded him, and he was my father, that means I'm a time jumper or whatever you call yourselves?"

Sean sighed. "There are other reasons why I think that."

"Like what?"

"As a kid you used to...*hop* sometimes."

"What do you mean, *hop*?"

"I'd put you in bed and tuck you in and then I'd go back out to my chair—"

"And?"

"And you'd already be out there, sitting in *your* little chair, waiting for me."

Broch snorted a laugh. "That's adorable."

Catriona turned on him. "What are you laughing at? You're in the same boat as me."

He scowled. "Ah'm nae."

"You *are*. You came here and you don't even

know how."

Broch grunted.

Catriona rubbed her eye with the palm of her hand. "I don't understand any of this. I don't *hop* now. If what you say is true, why can't I do it now?"

Sean shrugged. "I don't know. I can't hop around either. Maybe it's a kid thing."

"I'm starting to wonder who *isn't* a time traveler. At the very least, we seem to be drawn to each other." Catriona recalled reading in Sean's journal how his wife—presumably Broch's mother—had been murdered and a thought occurred to her. "Do you think your wife is alive? Maybe she jumped, too?"

Sean shook his head. "Brochan's mother wasn't one of us."

"How do you know?"

"I buried her, for one."

"Oh." She looked at Broch. "Maybe that's why Broch doesn't remember anything from his past and you do. Because he's half human?"

Sean barked a laugh, causing heads to turn. He sobered and cleared his throat, leaning across the table to speak more softly to Catriona.

"You think I'm not *human*?" he asked.

She shrugged. "It's not like you're *normal*. Who knows?"

Sean put his hand on hers. "Cat, we're human."

"But how do you explain what you do?"

"I can't. I think we're just not as *rooted* as other people."

"And that's it? We can travel through time? We

don't fly or have super strength or anything?"

Sean chuckled. "No. From what I can tell we don't have superpowers other than a pathological need to help people in trouble."

"Really?"

"Really. I didn't become a studio fixer by accident. I think trouble is attracted to us, and we're better at dealing with it than most."

Catriona sighed. "I'd rather be able to fly."

Sean sighed. "Well, for what it is worth, you've got your memory."

"What about my memory?"

"The way you picture things so clearly. I think it's an offshoot of your time traveling abilities. I think we can mentally hop into the past to peek at what we're trying to remember."

"You mean I'm *literally* jumping back to the time I saw whatever it is I'm trying to remember?"

"Yes. In a fashion. I'm able to do it as well. Your ability is stronger than mine, though. I think of it as peeking through time's curtain."

Catriona arched an eyebrow. "Peeking through time's curtain? My, that's poetic."

"Thank you."

She hooked a thumb toward Broch. "How do you explain him not even remembering where he came from?"

Sean considered Broch. "He's young?"

Catriona set her jaw and stared into Sean's eyes. "There—I just pictured my kitchen in my head. Did I disappear? Did I flicker?"

Sean shook his head. "I don't think it happens like that—"

She raised her hands in frustration. "Then how *does* it happen?"

"I don't have all the answers. It's not like I had a meeting with the time-traveling king and he told me how this works. My best guess is that time isn't as linear as people think and we're able to exploit that. Einstein was on to something, there. It would help if you read a book on String Theory—"

Catriona dropped her forehead to the table. She remained that way until she heard Broch's voice, soft and soothing.

"Dae ye want some breid?"

She turned her head sideways to see him. He peered back at her from inches away.

"No, thank you, Broch. I don't think *breid* will make me feel any better right now."

He nodded and leaned back. Glancing at the basket he'd pushed to the back of the table, he again leaned forward to whisper to her.

"Kin ye git me some, then?"

Ignoring him, she sat up and pointed at Sean. "All those trips."

"What?"

Heads turned. She winced and tried again to find a more controlled tone. "All those trips you've taken. You always refused to take me. They weren't for work, were they? You were time traveling?"

"No—they were normal work trips. I told you, I can't just hop back in time, kill Hitler, and then show up in time for dinner."

Catriona suffered a rising frustration. "How could you not have told me? You told *him* a couple days after he showed up. Why—"

Sean took her hand. "This isn't the life I wanted for you, Cat. I wanted to spare you the danger. I hoped by helping me with my studio work you'd satisfy the urge."

"Satisfy what urge?"

"I told you. We're drawn to help people. I thought if you helped the studio you wouldn't be pulled to do other work. Work I couldn't control."

"But—" Catriona's phone buzzed. Sean's came to life a second later.

"Amber Crane," said Sean, reading his caller ID.

"Her husband," said Catriona, checking her own.

Sean stood. "See? Trouble even finds us at dinner."

They left Broch at the table and wandered outside.

Catriona answered as she walked. "Owen? What's wrong?"

The man on the other end of the line shouted back at her. "Someone's taken my son! They took Toby!"

She jerked the phone away from her ear to avoid hearing loss. "Easy, Owen, calm down. I can barely understand you. Is that Amber in the background?"

She heard him take a deep breath. "Yes. She called Sean."

"I'm with Sean now. You're sure Toby's been taken? Remember Amber left him with her mother that one time—"

"No—this is different."

"Have you called the police?"

"Amber wanted to but I wasn't sure—"

"Call them. And we'll be there as soon as we can."

Catriona disconnected and saw Sean was still on the phone. She returned to their table and caught the eye of the waiter.

"I'm so sorry, but there's been an emergency and we need to leave. Can you bring me the check for the drinks?"

"And the lava cake," said the waiter.

"And the what?"

The waiter peered down his nose at Broch and Catriona saw the Highlander's lips were covered by a dark smear.

"Someone helped himself to the dessert tray," said the waiter.

"Telltale," muttered Broch.

Catriona followed the waiter's attention to a tray sitting against the wall behind Broch. On it, sat an empty plate amongst the dessert examples.

"You ate the cake off the dessert tray?" she asked Broch.

"Ah only took *one* lik' Sean said, nae the whole tray."

She handed the waiter her credit card. "Bill me for the drinks *and* the lava cake."

The waiter sniffed and with one last sideward glance at Broch, strode away.

Broch watched him go, his eyes narrowing.

"That's not a buffet," whispered Catriona.

He pulled his attention away from the retreating server. "Buffet? That's French. It tasted French. T'was a wee dry, though."

"It's a *sample dessert*. It's probably been sitting on that tray for a week."

Broch's lip curled. "Och."

Catriona took a deep breath and made a conscious effort not to expend her agitation with Sean on the Highlander. He didn't know any better. And the cake had looked good. She'd eyed it herself once or twice.

"It's okay. We'll teach you all this fancy stuff later. For now, we've got to go."

The waiter returned and Catriona signed for the bill. Broch rose to his full height. He scowled at the waiter, whose eyes now danced everywhere *but* in the direction of the Scotsman.

When Catriona finished signing, the waiter snatched the receipt from her and scurried off.

"Aye, ye run, wee man," said Broch.

The other diners' heads swiveled, gazes dropping to Broch's kilt, and Catriona grabbed his wrist, tugging him toward the door.

CHAPTER TEN

Catriona, Broch and Sean arrived at Owen Crane's house to find they'd beaten the police. The Cranes had recently separated, with rumors of infidelities on both sides. Owen's wife, Amber, had once been one of Parasol Picture's top earners, a breakout star in the college comedy *Frat Brat*. She'd worked less as it became more difficult to believe her in the role of a sexy college student. A tragic collagen lip injection blunder that left her duck-faced for months hadn't helped.

Amber and Owen stood at the end of the driveway waving them forward as they piled from the car. Amber ran forward and threw her arms around Sean as he approached.

"They took Toby," she wailed.

"Who took him?" asked Sean, offering her a quick squeeze and then peeling away.

"I don't know." She noticed Broch in his kilt and wiped her eyes. "You brought an actor with you?"

"He works for me," said Sean.

Amber's face pinched as she appeared to ponder what working for Sean had to do with kilts. After a moment, she bobbed one shoulder as if to admit defeat.

Sean touched her arm. "Show me where you last saw Toby."

She nodded and glared at her husband before heading for the stairs. "This is *his* fault."

Owen followed. "Don't *start*. Now is not the time to start this *crap*."

They mounted the stairs and entered the home Owen had rented after his separation. Inside, Owen found a spot in the middle of the living room. Hands out at his sides, as if he were preparing to catch a medicine ball, he pivoted toward each location as he listed them.

"Okay. I was in the shower. Toby was out here watching TV."

"You were alone?" asked Sean.

Owen nodded. Amber arched an eyebrow and huffed.

Catriona wandered around the room, listening as Sean questioned Owen. She walked to the back of the house and peered through the sliding doors.

A pool.

She pointed to it through the glass. "You checked the, uh..."

Eyes swiveled toward her.

"First place I looked," said Owen.

Amber nodded. "And the first place I looked when he called me."

Catriona walked outside as Sean continued his interview with Owen. Broch followed. She wandered once around the pool and touched a towel crumpled on a chair. It was wet. The grout lines between the tiles were also wet near the stairs that led into the pool.

"Did you step into the water?" she asked Broch.

He shook his head. "Na. It's tempting though. Ah lik' Sean's pool."

Catriona returned to the towel and pinched the edge of it to lift it. Something dropped from it and rolled away toward Broch's toes.

"Whit's that?"

"Don't touch—"

Her warning came too late. He bent and picked up the small, white object before Catriona could stop him.

Broch's eyes grew wide, like a child caught in the act of something naughty. He held the item out to her. "Sorry."

"Remind me to explain fingerprints to you," she said, holding out her open palm.

He dropped the object into it and she rolled it around her hand.

"Whit is it?" he asked.

"Wireless ear bud. You put them in your ears and you listen to music."

"Na...really?"

She nodded.

Retracing her steps toward the house, Catriona found a small puddle outside the sliding door that she'd missed on the way out.

She slid open the door and reentered the house with Broch on her heels.

"Did you go swimming this morning?" she asked.

Owen turned to her and put his hand on his chest.

"Me? No."

"What about Toby?"

"He's not allowed in there without me."

"There's a wet towel out there and a puddle by the stairs."

Amber's head snapped toward her estranged husband. "Was Toby in the pool without you?"

"No." Owen scratched his head, his face twisted in what looked like confusion. "Oh, you know what? I think I did take a quick dip. Early. I was thinking that was yesterday but it was this morning."

"You lost an ear bud," said Catriona, holding it out to him.

He reached out and she dropped it into his hand. "Oh...thanks."

Amber scowled. "You don't use ear buds."

He shrugged. "Sure I do."

"No you—ohmygod. *She* was here, wasn't she?"

Owen's eyebrows rose. "What?"

Catriona could see from his overtly guileless expression that Amber had hit upon the truth. Owen never had been much of an actor.

Amber shook her head and crossed her arms over her chest. "Unbelievable."

"Who else was here?" asked Sean.

Owen caved, shoulders slumping. "My girlfriend was here earlier. But she was gone by the time Toby went missing."

"I knew it," hissed Amber. "You left Toby alone while you were plowing that old *tramp*."

"Amber, I told you. I was *alone* and in the shower.

Fiona had been gone an hour or more and Toby was watching cartoons. What, am I supposed to tie him to the toilet every time I take a shower?"

"He's *eight*."

Owen took a step towards her, his fists clenching. "You left him with your mother and forgot where he was when he was *three*."

"I knew he was safe."

"Was he? Your mother is a—"

"All right," said Sean, stepping between them. "Blaming each other isn't going to help anything."

There was a knock on the door and Catriona turned to see a woman standing behind the screen door, peering in.

"Who's that?" she asked, moving to the door.

Owen glanced at the door and then closed his eyes, waiting a beat before answering. "That's Fiona."

Catriona saw Broch's head swivel. He took a step forward as if to get a better view of the visitor, nearly bumping into her as she made her way to the door. Her own curiosity piqued by his, Catriona studied the woman. A tall, lithe and ravishing woman of about thirty-five, Fiona's dark hair was cut short and sassy.

Owen's squeeze seemed familiar, but Catriona couldn't fathom the reason why until she realized Fiona was the woman whose face had been splashed across the tabloids around the time the Cranes' marriage fell apart.

Fiona Duffy.

She realized Fiona was staring back at her.

No one had said a word.

"Come in, Fee," said Owen.

Like a hypnotist had snapped his fingers, the two dark-haired women both leapt into action. Catriona took a step back and Fiona entered to brush past her.

"I came as fast as I could," said Fiona taking her place beside Owen. She wrapped her hand around his.

Owen glanced at Amber and slid his hand from Fiona's, under the guise of needing to scratch his chin.

Amber tossed her auburn hair, her expression twisted tight as a knot.

Catriona noticed Broch's attention hadn't left the new woman. She *was* striking, with large blue eyes, high cheekbones and a playful smirk that never seemed to leave her lips. Catriona mused that Fiona felt a little like a 2.0 version of herself, similar in hair color, shape and stature, but with all the extra time and planning it took to represent as an actor in Hollywood. After all, she might be photographed by paparazzi at any moment.

Catriona was more of a throw-on-jeans-and-go sort of girl.

Broch's brow furrowed. Fiona glanced at him, noticed him staring, and smiled. The side of Broch's mouth twitched in response.

Catriona took a step toward him, but before she could say anything, there was another knock on the door and two uniformed policemen entered. Amber ran to them, begging them to find her son.

Sean nodded to Catriona, indicating that it was time to go. He shared some final thoughts with Owen and one of the officers as she and Broch headed outside.

Catriona glanced one last time at Fiona. The woman watched her leave without showing the slightest reaction to her stare.

Catriona and Broch didn't get far before one of the officers outside asked them to identify themselves. Before she could answer, another officer hit the first on the arm with the back of his hand.

"It's Cat. She works for the studio. She's okay," he told his partner.

Catriona smiled and nodded, thanking him for saving her the trouble of explaining herself.

"He's with me," she said, jerking a thumb towards Broch.

The officers eyed the Highlander's kilt and smirked at each other before heading up the stairs to the Cranes' home.

Another police car arrived and a young woman with brown hair, gripping a note book to her chest, appeared. Looking determined and stressed, she pushed past them and headed for Owen's door. Her head swiveled, her long silver earring swinging against her head, to gawk at Broch's kilt before she entered.

Moving about town with Broch was starting to feel like traveling with an alien by her side.

Maybe it was.

"You're really going to have to learn to love jeans. Maybe we could try some shorts," said Catriona as they wandered toward the car.

He didn't respond. She looked up at him, finding his silence unusual.

"Hey, what was up with that woman?" she asked.
He snapped out of his trance. "Whit?"

"That woman, Fiona. You were staring at her."

"Och, was ah?" He shook his head. "Ah was thinkin'—the boy—it's someone they ken."

Something about Broch's expression gave her the impression he was hiding something, but his opinion on the kidnapping rang true. She'd been thinking the same thing.

"I agree. Let me ask you—why do you think so?"

"Na yin broke in. They *walked* in."

Catriona nodded, impressed. "Good observation. Though, he told Sean the doors were unlocked. It could have been anyone."

"Brave tae donder in lik' that, dinnae ye think? Thay knew na yin was in the hoose except the da. They knew he was in the shower."

"So it was someone he knows, or someone who's been watching."

Broch squinted, searching the street. "Aye. Mibbiee *watching*."

She heard Sean saying his good-byes to the officers and he soon joined them by the curb.

"Broch says it's an inside job," said Catriona.

"Agreed," said Sean as they entered the Jag.

Catriona slapped her hands on her thighs. "Well, we should probably pop back through time, huh? We can stand outside Owen's door and stop whoever took Toby."

Sean rolled his eyes. "It doesn't work that way."

"A lot of good that does us."

She glanced back at Broch and found him staring back at Owen's house.

CHAPTER ELEVEN

Broch didn't know how to describe the feeling that came over him upon meeting Owen Crane's girlfriend.

Elated. Tingly. Confused.

Embarrassed.

The moment he heard the dark-haired woman's name, his dream came rushing back to him. The girl on a horse, the two of them galloping across the glen.

The love he'd felt for that girl was undeniable. He could feel his excited expectation at the prospect of spending time with her, as sure as he could feel his steed rising and falling beneath him.

Fiona.

Could Owen's girlfriend be *his* Fiona? Had he traveled through time to be reunited with his lost love?

He dropped his head into his hands.

"Are you okay?" asked Catriona.

He looked up to find Catriona peering at him from her place in the front passenger seat.

"Aye."

She smiled "You were quiet for nearly three minutes. I thought maybe you'd died."

"Ah'm well."

It was a lie. His heart ached. His feelings for Catriona were undeniable, but now—he wondered if his feelings had been misplaced.

Who is Fiona?

Broch heard a jingle and Catriona retrieved her phone to read a message.

She huffed. "I can't believe this. All I want to do is get back to our conversation—not to mention our dinner—and Jimmy Faxon needs me. Something about a dog bite."

Broch recalled Faxon's name from the book Catriona had made for him. She'd written a few words on all the studio's actors to help him learn his job more quickly. Jimmy Faxon was a musician turned actor currently starring in what Fiona had called *an evening cop-drama/soap-opera* called *Detroit Blues.*

Sean pulled onto the highway. "What can *you* do about a dog bite? Call Noseeum."

Catriona slipped her phone back into her pocket. "Faxon's not the one who was bitten. *His* dog bit the neighbor, who threatened to have the dog taken away and destroyed. Jimmy proceeded to then hit the neighbor with his guitar."

Sean groaned. "Please tell me it wasn't the guitar the studio loaned him. The one signed by Prince that they used in last week's episode?"

"He didn't say. But he did call it *the purple guitar.*"

Sean's chin dropped to his chest. "That boy never fails to confirm everything I suspect about him."

"When are we going to get back to our meeting?" asked Catriona.

Sean glanced at Catriona. "I didn't have anything else to share, anyway."

"Oh, *yes you do*. I'm not out of questions, so you're not out of answers."

Sean changed lanes. "We're an exit away from Jimmy's. I'll drop you off."

"Dae ye need me?" asked Broch.

Catriona twisted to face him. "Not technically. Are you sure you're okay? You look pale."

He squinted one eye. "Ah suppose ah'm nae feeling well."

"Might be the week-old lava cake. It's okay. I'll take this one. I *did* do this without you for *years* after all."

Catriona stared pointedly at Sean as she said her last sentence, and Broch felt even worse. Catriona hadn't ask for him, and now he worried the romance he'd felt blossoming between them might be built upon his own confused recollections.

He sighed. He was nothing but a nuisance to her. She didn't deserve to be saddled with him.

Sean pulled off the freeway and delivered Catriona to Jimmy Faxon's house. A man with blond hair and a square patch of black hair on his chin stood outside arguing with a heavy-set brown-skinned man. In the blonde man's arms, a tiny, white dog yapped endlessly.

"Wish me luck," said Catriona hopping out of the car.

Sean turned to Broch. "Why don't you come up front? Sometimes riding in a back seat can make a person sick."

Broch switched places and Sean headed for the studio.

"While we're alone, do you have any questions? Catriona has a way of being *heard*. I hope she didn't keep you from asking something you wanted to know," said Sean.

It took Broch a moment to register what Sean had said. "Whit? Ah—no..."

"Are you sure? You keep looking at me like you're working up the nerve to ask me something."

Broch sighed. "Och. Aye, ah dae hae somethin' tae ask."

"Go ahead."

Broch took a moment to run his tongue over his teeth as he tried to find a way to pose his inquiry.

Best tae say it.

He blurted out his thoughts before he could second guess them. "Dae ye ever hae dreams aboot yer past?"

"You mean about *being* in the past?"

"Aye."

Sean nodded. "All the time."

"Dae ye dream aboot things ye forgot?"

"Sure."

"And all yer dreams...they're true?"

"You mean did my dreams really happen?"

"Aye. Are they fantasies? Or memories come at nicht?"

Sean frowned. "I don't know. I imagine they're like any other dream. Sometimes they're true memories and sometimes they're a collection of things...memories, fantasies, wishes. The truth lies somewhere in between."

Broch considered this. His head believed his dreams were fantasy, but his heart told him otherwise.

"Did you dream about something specific?" asked Sean.

Broch shrugged. "A few things."

"But something in particular is bothering you?"

"Aye. A lassie. Someone ah may have loved."

Sean grimaced. "Oh. I could see how that might be upsetting."

Broch knew Sean had lost his wife in another time. He decided there remained no reason to hold back the full breadth of his concerns.

"Ah'll be honest, Sean. Ah hae feelin's fer Catriona. Ah dae. But the lassie in mah dreams... Ah'm worried..."

"That somewhere your wife is waiting for you?" finished Sean.

Broch sighed. "Aye. My Fiona."

Sean chuckled "Fiona? Like Owen's girlfriend?"

"*Very much* like Owen's girlfriend," said Broch.

His tone must have conveyed his meaning. Sean turned to look at him.

"Oh," he said. "*Oh.*"

"Dae ye know if she's one of us?"

Sean shook his head. "No. Are you sure you dreamt about *her*? Maybe you're just attracted to her? She's a beautiful woman."

Broch dropped his head into his hands with a great expelling of breath.

"Ah dinnae ken."

Sean patted him on the arm. "Keep the heid, son."

Broch nodded. "Keep the heid."

CHAPTER TWELVE

1833 - Edinburgh, Scotland

"Aff tae find Gavin, Da," called Brochan, splashing water from a barrel across his sweaty torso.

After rinsing the soot from his face and body, he changed into his best kilt and donned a clean shirt. The fabric strained against his biceps. Working as an apprentice blacksmith for his father had encouraged his arms to outgrow his sleeves. He'd been meaning to buy a new one, but there was never enough time in a day.

"Da?"

Broch checked to be sure his father wasn't lurking nearby. Finding himself alone in their small establishment, he pulled a sword from behind a stack of hay. Forbidden to forge a sword until deemed ready, he'd been crafting the weapon on the sly, whenever his father left the shop.

Unsure of his own exact age, Broch guessed he was somewhere past twenty. His father had found him, unconscious and abandoned as a boy. He remembered nothing about his life before awakening beside the kindly blacksmith's fire. They declared the day he was found, his birthday—age unknown.

He spent most days pounding out nails, pot hooks, spatulas, horseshoes and other mundane hardware, while his adopted father spent countless hours creating the finest blades in Edinburgh.

As a full-grown man, he *deserved* to create something more interesting than a pot hook.

He suspected he knew why his father restricted sword-making. He didn't want Broch to fall in love with the trade. No one would remain a blacksmith if faced with a lifetime of horseshoe bending. But crafting a sword—that inspired a man to obsess on the ways he might improve his blades.

Making a sword would make him a blacksmith.

His father didn't want him to be a blacksmith. It was good, honest work, but made for a hard life. His father's friend, Gregor Logan, was a landed man whose son Gavin was, almost by default, Broch's best friend. Laird Logan allowed Broch to school with his son's private tutors. Thanks to Laird Logan, the blacksmith was able to dream of a better life for Broch.

Out of necessity, his father trained Broch how to run the forge. He needed the help. But Broch spent much of his time studying with Gavin.

He was *a gentleman in training*, as his father liked to say.

Thanks to the Logan family's generosity, Brochan could read and write, spoke a little French and knew how to act in polite company.

In return, Broch kept wild Gavin grounded and watched his back.

He'd see Gavin tonight, but it wasn't a time to study. Tonight, Broch planned to meet Gavin at The Sheep Heid Inn and unveil his masterpiece.

Broch wrapped a cloth around the sword and, calling out a quick good-bye to the empty house behind the shop, slipped away.

The inn wasn't far. Tonight, it boasted a crowd, but he spotted Gavin already sitting at a table, draining his mug. Broch ordered a pint at the bar and joined his friend.

"Howfur far ahead of me are ye," he asked, sitting.

Gavin grinned. "This is mah first. Kin ye ever be on time, man?"

"Sorry. We cannae *all* spend our days roamin' aroond our da's mansion. Some of us hae tae work."

Gavin leaned forward and tried to smack Brochan on the head. The bigger man easily dodged the attempt, and slapped his friend on the ear before he could retreat.

"Ye'll be sorry if ye huv a go at that again."

Unafraid, Gavin grinned and rolled his eyes.

Broch pulled the covered sword from beneath the table and opened the cloth.

"Keek whit ah brought tae show ye."

Gavin gaped at the weapon. "Yer da made it?"

"*Ah* made it. Whit dae ye think?"

Gavin examined the blade, lifting it to feel its heft and balance. "She's bonny fer certain."

"She better be. Ah've been workin' on her a year."

Beaming, he tilted back his pint and caught the stare of a young woman sitting with an older man on the opposite side of the room. He nodded and she looked away, but soon glanced back, long enough for him to detect a smile on her lips.

Gavin slapped him on his arm. "She has eyes on ye."

"Who is she?"

"Ah dinnae ken her. Ah ken him, though. Mah da spoke tae him about some transaction. He's an American. Mr. Jones ah think his name was. Mebbe she's his daughter?"

"Or his young wife."

Gavin laughed. "No wonder her eyes are roamin' —she's in need of a young buck."

Broch grunted and looked down at his beer. "She's bonny ah suppose."

"Aye. Ah think she was keekin' at *me*. Ah lik' me a restless young bride nae and again."

Broch arched an eyebrow. "Ye would hae better luck with a restless young *sheep*."

Gavin burst into ale-fueled laughter. Looking past Broch, the grin melted from his face.

"Ludo is here," he said.

Broch heard a voice behind him.

"Och, the fancy boys are here."

He turned to find a familiar lout staring down at him, mug in his hand. Ludo Wilson was a local bully. Broch assumed him to be drunk. He'd never had the nerve to try his luck when sober.

"Whit dae *ye* want?" asked Broch.

Ludo sneered and turned away.

Broch returned his attention to Gavin. "Eejit," he

muttered.

Gavin nodded in agreement before returning his concerns to his ale.

The two young men exchanged stories of their day until Broch heard a woman's voice rise over the din of the pub, demanding to be left alone.

He peered over the people sitting beside them, spotting the girl whose eye he'd caught earlier in the evening. Her gentleman companion had disappeared.

In his place, sat Ludo.

Broch rose.

"Dinnae get into it with Ludo," said Gavin, leaning back his head. "Ah dinnae feel lik' helpin'."

"Ah won't need yer help," said Broch. He could see Ludo had his hand around the girl's wrist, effectively pinning her to the table as he leaned in, his face close to hers.

"Watch my sword," he said to Gavin, before pushing through the crowd.

The girl's eyes found his, her expression strained as she struggled to free her hand from Ludo's grasp. Her panic seemed to grow, and Broch realized that as far as she knew, he was her aggressor's partner. He sped his advance to ease her concern.

"Let her go," he said, arriving table-side.

Ludo looked up at him, his expression darkening. "Piss off."

Broch grabbed the man by the back of his shirt and jerked him to his feet. Ludo yelped, closed his eyes and raised his hands, expecting to be struck. When nothing happened, he unscrewed his eyes to stare up at Broch, who remained still, glaring at him. Ludo wobbled, uneven on his feet, and swiveled to scan the room, which had grown quiet.

Broch watched Ludo's gaze sweep the inn and spoke. "Yer friends aren't here tae help ye. Ah've seen them. T'wouldn't matter if they were."

"Who dae ye think ye are?" mumbled Ludo with half-hearted bravado.

"Get on with ye, before ah break your thick heid on this table."

Ludo took a step away, turned to leave, and then looked over his shoulder. "Ye'll pay for this."

"Ah doubt it." Brochan pushed him toward the door and he stumbled forward, knocking into several patrons who offered shoves of their own.

After a smattering of laughter, the roar of conversation resumed in the inn.

Broch turned his attention to the young woman, only to find the older gentleman had reappeared and reclaimed his seat. He was tall and wiry, his eyes so light blue they could pass for white. The man's sunken countenance suggested to Broch that he might break down a sheep's carcass using only the man's cheekbones for knives.

"Can I help you?" asked the man. His accent sounded strange, until he remembered Gavin mentioning that he was an American.

Broch glanced at the young woman and she looked down. The man's icy glare never wavered.

Broch shook his head. "Na."

He returned to his table to find Gavin sitting with

a dirty-blonde girl, his face buried in her neck. The girl giggled as he approached and his friend glanced up from his sloppy business.

"Och, Brochan, have ye met Machara?"

Brochan nodded his greeting. He'd heard the name *Machara* before and knew that it translated to *plain*. The girl herself had tried to argue against that life sentence. Her face glowed with the blush of artificial enhancements, her dress and hair woven with ribbons and baubles meant to catch the eye. He could tell from the depth of her makeup she'd suffered smallpox scars, though she'd fared the disease better than most.

All these things told him he'd lost Gavin's attention for the evening.

"Are ye stayin'?" asked Gavin. His tone implied the answer he hoped to hear.

Machara offered him a saucy smirk and patted the bench beside her. "Aye, have a seat and stay a spell."

Broch shook his head. "Na. Ah've got somethin' to dae."

Gavin scowled. "Somethin' to dae?"

"Aye. I embarrassed Ludo. By noo he's gathered his friends ootdoors tae lie in wait for me. Ah need tae give them their chance."

"Ye want help?"

"Na. Ah could use the practice. I'll see ye in th'morra."

Gavin nodded once and buried his face in the bosom of his companion. She shrieked with glee.

Brochan gathered his sword and walked to the bar.

"Hold my sword a moment, will ya, Andy?" he said, thrusting the wrapped weapon at the bartender.

Andy put a hand on the weapon and then nodded at the door. "Ludo's waitin' fer ye ootside. Ye micht wantae keep it."

Broch smiled. "That's why ah'm givin' it tae ye. Ah micht kill him as it is. With that, there'd be na doubt ah'd spend mah life in jail."

Andy nodded and slipped the sword behind the bar.

Broch turned to the exit and took a deep breath. *Eejits.*

He wasn't one to look for a fight, but Ludo and his band of thugs had been growing bolder in recent months, their childish mischief developing a sinister undertone. Between the crowd and the presence of her companion, chances were slim that the lassie in the inn was in any real danger. But what about the next fair creature? One Ludo cornered alone?

No, Ludo needed a reminder that not everyone was willing to turn a blind eye.

Flinging open the door Brochan stepped outside and immediately squatted to his heels.

There was a crash as wood splintered down on him like rain.

Brochan glanced up. A carrot-topped boy had swung a heavy branch at his head. The rotten limb had shattered against the door frame.

He'd anticipated the attack.

Ludo's friends weren't the most creative brutes.

Brochan reached out, grabbed the boy's boot and

launched himself upward, dragging the foot with him. With a yelp, the redhead flipped onto his back. Brochan raised his right arm in time to block a punch directed at his nose, catching it neatly in his palm. He locked eyes with Ludo.

"Ludo, dae we hae tae dae this? Can't ye just behave lik' a man?"

Ludo sneered. "Ye think ye'r sae much smarter than the rest o' us fur ye hae yer fancy friend."

Brochan snorted a laugh. "Ah dinnae think ah'm smarter than ye, fur o' Gavin. Ah think ah'm smarter than ye, fur ye hae the brains of a goat."

Another man with a flop of sandy-colored hair appeared from the darkness and struck Brochan on the jaw. Releasing Ludo's fist, Brochan fell back against the door frame.

A patron on his way out opened the inn door, peered at him, and quickly shut the door again.

Brochan rubbed the back of his hand across his lips and found blood. He grinned.

"A' richt then. *Let's play.*"

He recognized the sandy-haired man as Ludo's toady, Shaw, a short but powerful boy. Shaw raised his fist to swing again as the carrot-top grabbed Brochan's leg. Broch used his opposite leg to kick the ankle-biter, sending him sprawling on his back once more. The twist of his body caused Shaw's second strike to glance his shoulder.

Ludo took the opportunity to jump on Brochan's back. Feeling the weight, Broch whipped his left shoulder, tossing his foe into Shaw, who stumbled back several steps.

Ludo hit the ground.

"Dinnae stand there, hit him!" screamed Ludo, scrambling to stand.

Shaw glanced toward where Brochan had last seen the redhead laid out like a table cloth. He followed that gaze expecting to see the carrot-top rising.

The boy had disappeared.

Ludo found his feet and lunged one step toward Brochan before he realized Shaw had abandoned the fight. Both he and Broch watched Shaw stride away at a brisk clip.

"Coward!" Ludo screamed. Shaw made no movement to imply he heard or cared what Ludo thought of him.

"There's nae point tae this," said Broch to his remaining foe.

Ludo pointed to the inn. "Ye mocked me in there."

"Ye weren't being a gentleman. If yer goin' tae be a bore, ye'll be treated as such."

Ludo grimaced, his jaw clenched tight as he poked a finger in Broch's direction.

"Ye'll git yers," he spat, before storming off.

Broch sighed. A sliver of light fell on him and he glanced at the inn entrance to find the raven-haired girl had stepped outside. Her ghostly companion was nowhere to be seen.

"That was quite a thing. I could see it all from the window," she said.

He shrugged. "He's started somethin' with me

every couple of months since we were wee laddies. T'was time fer a reminding."

She smiled and he felt himself blush. Tasting metal, he licked the corner of his mouth and wiped at it. Finding blood on his hand, he dragged it against his kilt, attention locked on the pattern of his tartan to avoid staring directly into her eyes.

"Are ye new here then?" he asked as the silence grew deafening.

"I am."

"That man ye were sitting with. He's yer husband?" He sniffed and looked away, horrified that he'd asked such a forward question.

She giggled. "My father, silly."

"Ah."

He ran his hand through his hair and rocked on his heels. "Where'd ye travel fae?"

"London."

"But yer an American?"

"Yes. Is it that obvious?"

"Aye. Ye hae a confident way aboot ye. And, the way ye talk, of course."

"Of course."

"And...ye'll be staying 'ere for a spell?"

"As far as I know."

He nodded. "Hm."

"Did you grow up here?" she asked.

"Aye. Mostly. The man ah call my father took me in when ah was young. He's the blacksmith."

"So you know the area well?"

"Ah do."

Her eyes lit. "Maybe you could show us around some time? My father could use a guide—"

Her father burst from the pub looking harried. Upon seeing his daughter conversing with Brochan, he came up short and scowled, his thin lips drawing tighter.

"Come, Fiona!" he snapped before turning and striding down the road.

She flashed Broch an uneasy smile. "I have to go."

"Good nicht, Fiona," he blurted, as she turned to run after her father.

She stopped and turned. He could see the flush in her cheeks by the inn's lamplight.

"I didn't catch your name," she said, her voice more quiet than it had been.

"Brochan."

She smiled. "Good night, Brochan."

Broch watched her run after her father until a banging noise snapped him from his trance. He looked at the door to the inn. It shook as if someone pounded on the opposite side.

"Hello?"

The door rattled as the drumming resumed.

He reached out and wrapped his fingers around the iron handle—

With a gasp, Broch sat up in bed.

It was a dream.

Another dream about Fiona.

He closed his eyes and tried to picture her, managing only the spill of her dark hair and the flash of blue eyes. Her face remained more of an impression of beauty...an unfinished painting.

He felt ill.

My heart aches.

It was if his heart had swollen and now pushed against his ribs, demanding to be set free. His breath came in shallow sips, such was the pressure on his lungs.

The idea that he had spent time in eighteen-thirty-three made sense. Up until now, his only solid memories had been from the mid-seventeen hundreds—but he'd been a boy.

In this new dream, he'd been a man and an orphan.

He closed his eyes and recalled the memory he'd wanted to forget. The memory of finding the three women who served as his mothers, slaughtered. The man on horseback returning to kill him, swinging—

He opened his eyes.

Mibbie mah trip through time tae California wasn't mah first.

As a boy, he'd been wounded by the man who slaughtered his family. Of that much he was sure. He might have then jumped to eighteen thirty-three, where he'd been found by the blacksmith.

It fit so neatly. His time with Fiona *could* be a memory.

Not a dream.

He looked at his arms. They *were* large. He could have been a blacksmith. He rubbed his fingers, feeling the callouses there.

Ah could hae been a blacksmith.

If all that was true...

Fiona.

A banging echoed through the apartment. *Knocking.* The sound that must have awoken him.

Someone was at his door.

He scowled and ripped his sheets to the side. "Och, ah'm coming."

CHAPTER THIRTEEN

Broch opened the door, appearing agitated.

"Were you asleep?" asked Catriona.

He rubbed at his hair. "Aye. Well, na, ah'd just woken."

As his arm dropped he reached out to pinch the fabric of her blue pajama set, rubbing it between his fingers.

"They're silk," she said, taking a step forward. Once inside his apartment, she realized she'd taken his interest in her clothing as tacit permission to enter. He hadn't asked her to come in, and his expression appeared...pensive. Maybe even *annoyed*.

"Ah've *seen* silk," he said.

"Oh. Well, actually, they're not *real* silk. I don't think I paid enough for them. They're fake silk."

He closed the door behind her. "There are a lot of fake things aroond 'ere."

She chuckled and sat on the sofa. "We're in Los Angeles. You have no idea."

He sat down in a standalone chair facing her.

Way over there.

She glanced at the perfectly good seat beside her on the sofa.

Was it conceited to be offended he hadn't taken the

opportunity to be closer?

Everything felt a little off. She'd sensed it earlier in the car and blown it off, but now—

"Did ye come 'ere tae sit on mah furniture at midnight?"

She looked up and realized she'd been staring at the coffee table like an idiot.

"Sorry. No. I came to ask you what you thought about the stuff Sean told us."

"Lik' whit?"

"Like how we like helping people and trouble tends to find us?"

He scoffed. "Ah already ken that."

"Did you? I mean did you *really*, or are you joking?"

He hooked his mouth to the side. "A wee bit of both."

"Have you remembered anything else about before you came here?"

He looked away and shook his head. "Na."

There it is. He's lying. She could see his deceit as if his pants were literally on fire. Not that he was wearing pants. He had his sheet wrapped around his waist, tied artfully at the side. *How does he do that?* She could never get towels or sarongs to stay tied.

Oh for crying out loud what does that matter?
Stay focused.

The question on the table was *why is he lying?* He usually reveled in sharing with her what little of his past he could remember.

Or had he always remembered more than he shared?

"Catriona, 'tis late."

"Huh? Oh. I'm sorry. Hey, are you okay?"

He cocked his head to the side. "That means *good*, richt? Ye say it often."

"What?"

"Oh-kay."

"Oh, yes. It means all right. Good."

"Then aye, ah'm okay."

"You seem a little *off*."

He shook his head and stood. "Ah'm tired."

She jumped to her feet. "My bad. It was way too late to swing by. I thought maybe you were awake and I wanted to talk about what Sean said—I guess I said that already. Okay. I'm going to go."

He stared at her as if he had something to say. She wanted to push him to share, but felt equally sure that in his current mood, he'd find such encouragement an intrusion. Unnerved, she felt her expression bunch into a squinty smile she *knew* made her look like a crazy person. She headed for the door.

"I'll catch up with you tomorrow," she said.

"Aye."

He followed and, with a final nod, closed the door behind her.

Sad.

It struck her the moment she heard the door click. That was his expression. He looked *sad*.

She stood in the hallway staring at his door, before realizing his door had a peephole. She jumped away and pressed her back against the wall that stretched the distance between their apartments.

Smooth.

He'd probably spied her standing there, staring at his door like a puppy thrown outside after piddling on the rug, and then watched as she *freaked out* and disappeared.

She took a deep breath and wondered why Broch made her act like a school girl. Sure, he was smoking hot, but it was more than that. Something made him feel *important* to her.

She took a deep cleansing breath.

Or, maybe I'm just an idiot.

Catriona peeled herself from the wall and entered her own apartment, trying not to think about how strange the exchange with Broch had been. She tried extra hard to close her door without a sound.

Inside, she leaned against her wall and told herself not to over-think things. There were plenty of reasons Broch might seem out of sorts.

I woke him up.

He wasn't really all there.

He needed sleep or coffee.

She chuckled, remembering his attempt to make coffee at the hotel in Tennessee.

Glancing at the clock, she noted that it was a little after midnight. Not time for coffee.

Why am I so awake?

She clapped her hands together and looked around the apartment.

What to do, what to do...

She recalled Sean referencing her memory earlier in the evening.

If her memory was enhanced by an ability to bend time, wasn't it her duty to see if she could use it more proactively?

She moved into the kitchen and pulled a pad of paper from the drawer. Scribbling the alphabet on a sheet, she found scissors and proceeded to snip out each letter.

Scooping all the tiny pieces into her palm, she closed her eyes and dumped them on her island counter like alphabet confetti. She opened her eyes only long enough to *glimpse* at the scattered paper tiles, and then jogged into the bedroom.

Perched on her bed, she tried to picture the shower of paper squares. Some had landed face down, some face up. She closed her eyes and attempted to recall the visible letters.

The T was up.

She remembered that. The K and E were in the upper left of the pile, laying side by side. Those were the ones she remembered registering before she left.

She closed her eyes tighter.

There.

She could picture the pattern laying on the counter. The T, K, E...

The image in her mind became more clear.

Q, O, G, B, M, Y, R... one scrawled so poorly it might be an L or an I. She concentrated for a few more moments and then returned to the kitchen to study the pile.

They were there. All the letters she'd named were there, the others turned over so only the empty white backs remained visible. The pattern was how she'd remembered it.

"Ohmygod," she whispered to herself.

She didn't know how useful the trick could be, but it wasn't *not* cool.

She wanted to run and tell Kilty about it. Maybe see if he could do it—

Outside her front door, she heard the elevator doors open. Padding to the door she peeked outside in time to watch Broch step into the elevator, his body warped into a curve by her fisheye peephole lens.

The doors slid shut.

CHAPTER FOURTEEN

"Stop 'ere."

The car rolled to a halt and Broch stepped to the curb, a sense of accomplishment glowing like a fire in his chest.

He'd summoned a car without anyone's help.

While he was *clearly* an exceptional student, he still had Catriona to thank for his education. After much begging, she'd agreed to give him his own phone and demonstrated how to place calls, write texts and summon cars.

The twenty-first century wasn't so hard. But it *was* astonishing.

No longer did people need to keep and care for horses. Now they had horseless carriages propelling themselves across the terrain.

That's whit folk should call them, "horseless carriages."

He made a mental note to suggest that to whomever was in charge of such things. Catriona would know.

People didn't even have to drive their horseless carriages themselves. Press a button, and cars arrived with drivers already in them, waiting to escort people wherever they wanted to go.

He shook his head, marveling. It was all very

convenient.

Don't even git me started on the warm showers...

He walked two blocks and stopped upon recognizing Owen Crane's house. A low fence encircled the property, more decorative than useful. He hopped over the iron spikes, the jeans he'd worn for his evening mission tightening against his flesh. He preferred his kilt, but people stared less when he wore jeans and he didn't want to be noticed.

He tucked behind the large tree in Owen's yard, cloaked in darkness. When no one came running into the yard, and he felt sure he'd entered the property unobserved, he peeked around the trunk.

Lights glowed in Owen Crane's living room. Inside, he spied Owen and his girlfriend, Fiona, sitting close on the sofa. He felt a twinge of jealousy.

"Stop it," he hissed at himself.

A man whose serious expression identified him as an officer of some kind, sat in the corner of the living room looking bored. He had no interest in the couple sitting five feet away from his stiff-backed chair.

They're waiting fer the call.

Catriona had explained to him that Owen and his wife would each be waiting for a phone call from the person who took their child. Such a call would be welcome, considering the alternative. He understood. Except for the use of the telephone, kidnapping was something that hadn't changed since his day. The concept of people taken for ransom was as old as money itself.

Broch's gaze fell to the ground at his feet as a

feeling of remorse washed over him.

Catriona. He'd been rude to her. When she'd woken him from his dream he'd felt confused and helpless—two of his least favorite things to feel.

The woman in his dream had been so *real*. Even now he could feel what it was like to be near her.

Waking from that dream had felt like losing her.

Who is she? Had he disappeared from their bed, whisked to California, leaving her to wonder what had happened to him? And what were the chances that he would soon meet a strangely familiar woman by the same name?

As a rule he didn't believe in coincidence. Of all the years he might have visited, what brought him to *this* place and time? Sean, his father, was waiting for him in this future when he arrived. Who was to say his love was not?

The dream means something.

That's why he was hiding behind a tree, lurking like a bandit in Owen Crane's front yard. He hoped seeing Fiona again would answer questions. So far, staring at the back of her head through Owen's window, wasn't offering much in the way of illumination.

"Should I call the police?"

Broch jumped at the sound of the voice and ducked behind the tree, his back pressed against the bark. He grimaced.

Ye cannae hide now, eejit. Someone saw ye.

Peering around the trunk, he found a brown-haired woman, petite and pretty, holding a book against her chest and peering back at him. Broch guessed she'd exited the house through the back door and traveled the side path to where she now stood, staring at him.

She wasn't striking in the exaggerated way he'd found many of the women in the Los Angeles area, but she had a pleasant countenance. Her expression was one of amusement, not anger. Rolling from behind the tree, he glanced at the living room window to find Fiona and Owen had disappeared. The officer remained slouched in his chair, his arms crossed against his chest, head down.

Broch held out his hands, palms down in an attempt to demonstrate that he meant no harm. "Dinnae call the police."

"Why not?"

He struggled to find an acceptable excuse as to why he was lurking around Owen's front yard. Saying he'd come to stare at Fiona in order to divine if she was his long lost love would make him sound like a loon at best, a rogue at worst.

"You were here with Sean and Cat today," said the girl, blessedly filling the awkward silence.

He nodded. "Aye." *That's a reasonable excuse—ah'm working fer Sean.*

"Looking for evidence behind that tree?"

Now that's harder tae explain. Embarrassed, he felt his face flush and decided to be honest as possible. "No. Ah—it soonds strange, but ah had a dream."

She stepped forward and looked up at the second floor bedroom. Fiona now stood there in her bra, her body partially illuminated by dim light, her back to the window.

Och na.

The girl raised her eyebrows and looked at him. "A dream, huh? An X-rated dream?"

"Whit?"

"Your dream was about her? Fiona?"

He sighed and nodded.

The corner of the girl's mouth hooked to the side as she shook her head. Without saying a word, Broch felt as if she had scolded him.

"Ah'm not here tae hurt her."

"I would hope not."

"Ah mean, ah dinnae come tae keek at her."

The girl held up a hand. "I don't even want to know what that means."

Broch remembered Catriona hadn't known what *keek* meant either.

"Tae *look* at her. Ah mean ah wasnae tryin' tae catch her naked."

Something about his blunt confession made them both glance up at the window, just as Fiona turned toward them and unclasped her bra, dropping the garment to the ground.

Broch looked away and shook his head in defeat.

Why did she hae tae do that noo?

The girl chuckled. "Don't worry about it. It happens a lot. She has that effect on men. "

"Does she?" he asked.

She rolled her eyes. "You have no idea. She probably undressed in front of that window *because* she knew we were watching."

He grimaced. "She's bonny, aye, but ah wasn't after that. Ah think ah've met her afore."

She shrugged. "Deja vu? She's been in town a long time. You probably saw her on television."

"Mibbie. Ah have been peepin' a lot of that lately."

She tucked her notebook in one hand and thrust out the other. "My name's Asher. Well, it's *Kelly*, but my last name is Asher and that's what everyone calls me. I'm Owen and Fiona's assistant."

Broch shook. "Brochan."

She cocked her head, peering at his jeans. "Weren't you in a kilt earlier?"

"Aye."

"Why aren't you now? I thought that was pretty cool."

"Ah dinnae want tae draw attention tae myself."

"But you *did* want attention earlier?"

"Well, na, but—"

"So you're like, *Scottish* Scottish, huh?"

He squinted, unsure what she meant by saying the word twice. The woman talked too fast and he couldn't shake the feeling she was trying to trick him into admitting something incriminating.

She continued. "You guys are going to be looking into the kidnapping?"

"Aye. Ah believe sae."

She glanced back at the window and he followed her lead. Fiona had disappeared. His shoulders relaxed a notch. Asher and Fiona had him feeling like a scoundrel.

Asher tapped his arm and began to walk. "We should talk. Come with me. Where's your car?"

He followed. "Ah called one. It left."

"You like pie?"

"Pie?"

"Not shepherd's. You probably get enough of that in Scotland, huh? Ha. I meant, like, fruit and stuff. I know a 24-hour diner. Are you hungry?"

"Ah—"

"We'll go in my car. Come on."

She continued down Owen's path to the sidewalk and, at a loss for what else to do, he followed on her heels.

She drove them to a yellow building with a green roof that resembled a quaint home. Inside, they sat on a cushioned bench in front of a window that made him feel as if he perched in a picture frame for all the world to see. The improbable event of Catriona walking by and seeing him made him uneasy. He wasn't doing anything wrong, and yet everything felt improper.

Ah feel lik' a dog slipped aff his leash.

Asher pushed her menu aside. "What kind of pie do you like? They have all kinds here, apple, blueberry, pecan, lemon meringue—"

"Pecan?" The word struck him like a bolt of lightning. He rolled his tongue in his mouth, his taste buds tingling with the taste of what he knew to be pecans, but he couldn't place the time he might have eaten one.

Asher grinned. "Ooh, *pecan*. You've got a sweet

tooth." A server appeared and Asher handed her both menus. "He'll have the pecan and I'll take the lemon meringue."

Asher bent forward, nearly laying her head on the table to peer into Broch's eyes as he hung his head in thought.

"You okay?" she asked.

"Aye. Sorry. Ah think ah've had pecans afore but ah cannae mind where. Catriona says ah have, uh, *ambrosia*."

"Ambrosia?"

"Ah cannae mind things."

She laughed. "*Amnesia*. You're funny. You remind me a little of Owen. He's funny. I mean, usually. I don't think he feels like being funny now, with his kid missing and all. Are you and Catriona a thing?"

Broch tucked his chin and stared at Asher, marveling at how she shifted subjects without warning. "A *thing*?"

"You know. Dating. Bumpin' uglies. Sorry. That was crude. You know what I mean."

Broch shook his head. "No. Ah—Mibbie. Ah dinnae ken."

"Maybe? You're not sure if you're dating?" Asher laughed again, her startlingly white teeth flashing. "I love that accent of yours. Cat probably has a boyfriend though, right? She's super pretty. First thing I thought when I saw her this morning was *uh oh, Fiona's going to hate her*."

"How come would Fiona hate her?"

Asher rolled her eyes. "Fiona likes to be the

prettiest person in the room. Center of attention. You know—she's an actress, after all."

"But she and Owen—"

"He's just a stepping stone. He's too sweet for her. She's going to break his heart. You'll see. She's getting older and she thought she needed something comfortable, like a trusty old shoe, but I can tell she's already planning her next step."

Broch grunted. "Ye dinnae seem tae hae a very generous opinion of her."

Asher laughed. "No, I suppose I don't. She hasn't been my boss that long. I'm really Owen's assistant, but she's co-opted me." She took a sip of water before continuing. "Look at me, spilling all this to you. I don't even know you. But that's why I brought you here, you know, to talk about Fiona."

"Aye?"

Asher leaned toward him on her elbows, her voice dropping low. "She's up to something."

"Whit dae ye mean?"

"I don't know. I can't put my finger on it yet but the way she reacted to Owen's son being taken—I dunno. It was like she knew already."

"Did she ken, uh, *know* already?"

"I don't know how she could have. Unless, of course, she had something to do with it."

"Ye think *she* took the laddie?"

"Ha, *laddie*. That's hilarious. You are *so* Scottish. No. I—" She tossed back her head and left it there as she sighed. Lowering her chin, she locked eyes with him. "I'm sorry. I must sound ridiculous. Forget I said anything." She leaned forward again, her smile dropping beneath bedroom eyes. "Maybe I just wanted to ask you out for pie."

He froze, unsure of what to say, and she burst into laughter once more, throwing herself back against the seat so hard she bounced forward again before catching herself on the edge of the table.

"JK. You are hot, though. But not my type. Too manly. I like artists. How'd you get that scar next to your eye?"

He fingered the rugged tissue beside his left eye. Gaining that scar was the last memory he possessed of his previous life. He couldn't tell Asher that a man on horseback had slaughtered his mothers and then attacked him...

He shrugged. "A fight, ah think."

She nodded. "See? Too manly."

The waitress returned and placed a piece of pie in front of each of them. Asher grabbed her fork and scooped herself a mouthful before the waitress had a chance to leave. Broch lifted his fork and cut himself a chunk. The smell of it made him woozy.

He took a bite, the sugary filling coating his mouth. "'Tis sweet—"

It wasn't until he crunched on the first pecan that his memory exploded with images.

A girl. Dark hair. Laughing. The white skin of her throat exposed—

He placed his hands on his head.

"Hey, what's wrong?" asked Asher.

Asher's voice sounded miles away. He squinted,

the lights suddenly blinding.

"I have to go," he said, standing, his legs feeling weak beneath him.

"You don't like the pie?" she asked.

He grabbed the sticky treat from the plate with his hand. Half of it fell to the table as he held it aloft for her to see.

She scowled. "What the—"

Feeling ill, Broch forced a smile and ran from the restaurant.

He walked several blocks to be sure Asher didn't follow him, before collapsing against a building.

His head swirled with colors. A man approached, walking fast, his head down, hands in his pockets.

Broch grabbed his arm. "Where is this?" he asked.

"Hey!" The man jerked away, the whites of his eyes flashing.

"Where is this?" Broch repeated. "I need to call a car *here*."

The man scowled. "Dude, the phone knows where you are." He hurried away. Broch heard him spit some words he recognized as curses.

He peered down at his phone.

It kens where ah am?

Broch pressed the car calling button. It did, indeed, seem to know where he was. Earlier, he'd thought it knew his location because he was at the studio. Somehow, it seemed to *always* knew where he was.

He waited, breathing slow and deep to clear his mind. Several minutes later, a black sedan arrived.

"Hey, how ya doin'?" asked the driver as Broch opened the door.

Broch dismissed him with a wave. "Na blethering."

"What?"

"*Na talking.*"

"No talking. Okay, okay. I got it, buddy. I prefer that myself but they make us try and earn the damn stars."

His interaction with the driver took Broch's mind off the nonsense in his brain for a moment. His nausea passed. For that he was grateful.

Cradling the pecan pie in his hand, he closed his eyes and endeavored to block all sensory input for the remainder of the ride. When the driver turned on the radio Broch made a sharp barking noise and it went silent.

Broch felt the car roll to a stop and opened his eyes to find he'd reached the studio. He jumped out and jogged to his apartment, glancing at Catriona's door as he passed it. He didn't stop.

Safe at home, he yanked a plate from the kitchen cabinet and placed the chunk of pie on it. He washed the remaining sticky mess from his hands and carried the plate to his room.

Without changing from his clothes, he stretched on the bed like a dead man arranged for a wake.

Everything was quiet.

Only the familiar hum of the studio's security lights tickled his ears.

Once his breathing had reached a steady pace, he

reached with his left hand to pluck a single pecan from the pie.

He placed the nut in his mouth and sucked the sugar from it. It settled between his molars and, with a deep, expectant breath, he *crunched*.

CHAPTER FIFTEEN

1833 – Edinburgh, Scotland

Broch found his father's sleeping area empty.

The old blacksmith awoke earlier than the sun most days and often disappeared to enjoy a few hours fishing before spending a good part of the day in front of the fire, pounding steel.

Broch didn't blame him, but he could never understand how someone could stand on the edge of a loch for hours, waiting for something as dumb as a fish to bite.

Rubbing his neck he recalled the girl he'd met at the inn.

Fiona.

He'd dreamt about her. She'd kissed him, and he'd kissed her back.

Ridiculous.

She wasn't local. He'd probably never see her again.

He moved to the barrel where they kept water for washing. Keeping the barrel near the fire warmed the water and helped wash away the morning chill. He and his father kept the fire burning day and night.

Imagine if ah could wake in the morn' and bathe my whole

body in warm water.

He knew rich people sometimes took baths with water warmed by the fire. Some swore bathing opened the pores and let in sickness, but he didn't feel *sick* when he bathed. He felt *wonderful.* Bathing couldn't be wrong. He hoped to be rich enough to have servants draw him a bath each day, but knew there was little chance of that happening. Blacksmithing was an honorable trade, but not one likely to make him rich. Even if he stuck to his studies and became a teacher, he'd never have the money Gavin's father made as a trader.

Unfortunately, business and trade held little interest for Broch.

As he dried his face on a rough cloth, his mind wandered again to the previous night's dream. The soft brush of the girl's lips still lingered on his neck.

He threw down the towel.

Get to work, ye raver.

Stoking the fire, he prepared a piece of iron and pounded the metal, his hammer whistling through the air as he played his rhythmic beat.

If he couldn't have the woman in his dreams, at least he could wear himself out until he no longer cared.

The heat from the fire turned his flesh red. Sometimes, Brochan wished his adoptive father had been a farmer. For years, he'd had a recurring dream about tending a small plot of land for three older women. In each dream, the crops and seasons changed, but the women remained the same. So much so he'd come to feel as though he knew them as friends or mothers. In the dream, he liked working outdoors. The heat of the sun paled to the heat of the forge.

"I found you," said a voice.

Brochan glanced from his work, sweat stinging his eyes. He wiped his arm across his face and blinked to bring his vision into focus.

A young woman with dark hair stood at the door of his father's workshop.

Stepping back from the fire, he dipped the horseshoe on which he'd been working into a barrel of water. A dramatic burst of steam rose with an angry hiss and the girl yipped before breaking into giggles. The sound of her surprised whoop of laughter made him grin.

He recognized the girl from the inn—and his subsequent dream. Unwilling to appear too fervent to speak to her, he kept his face hidden from her and watched the steam rise for several seconds.

It's just a lassie. Keep the heid, man.

He took a deep breath and glanced over his shoulder, trying to appear as casual as possible.

"Ah ken *ye*. Yer the lassie from the inn."

She smiled. "And you're the *laddie* from the inn."

Feeling naked beneath her stare, he splashed water on his body and draped a cloth over his shoulder, across his chest. "Did ye need something? A horseshoe? A nail? Na, I ken—a sword?"

She chuckled. "No. I was in town and saw you here."

Really? Whit a coincidence. Ah just dreamt we made love beneath the stars.

He pressed his lips together and looked askance, finding it difficult to look into her eyes with such scandalous dreams running through his mind. Facing away from her, he felt emboldened, as if being unable to see her meant she could no longer see *him*.

"Have ye ever met someone, and thought fer sure ye'd met afore?" he asked, keeping his eyes riveted to the wall as he pretended to straighten his tools.

Her answer came quickly. "Yes. Have you?"

He turned and locked eyes with her. "Aye. Just yesterday, fer the first time. Dae ye think—"

Blushing a furious red, she looked down, pulling a white kerchief from a basket hanging from her arm. The kerchief was folded, creating what looked like a tiny sack.

"Have you ever had pecans?" she asked, cutting him short.

He noted her coloring and frowned.

Ah'm being tae forward. Ah'm terrifying the lass. Answer her question and let her change the subject.

"Ah've heard of them. Gavin—he was at the inn with me—he's had them afore."

"I did see you with another man at the inn. Where was that friend when you were attacked by those brutes?"

Brochan grinned. "Where he usually is. Far away and flirtin' with the lassies."

They stared at one another, dopey grins on their faces, until he felt the urge to straighten his tools once more. "Are ye sure ah can't make you something?"

Through furtive glances he watched her set the kerchief bundle on her hand and open the four corners to reveal several brown, rugged nuts.

"Would you like a pecan?" she asked.

He peered at her offering.

"Aye?"

She nodded. "My father has them sent from America."

"Would yer father lik' ye offering his American nuts tae a sweaty apprentice blacksmith?"

He regretted asking the moment the words left his mouth. He'd only meant to be funny, but it sounded as if he were accusing her of scandalous behavior.

She offered him a sly smile. "No. Perhaps not. But I find it best not to share everything with him."

Och.

Perhaps the rumor that American girls possessed uncommonly bold natures was true. But she wasn't lascivious, like Gavin's lassies.

No. The spark in Fiona's eye wasn't *flirtation.*

It was *defiance.*

Brochan took a deep breath.

Ah think ah love this lass.

Taking one of the pecans from her palm, he placed it in his mouth. Crunching, his mouth filled with a nutty flavor touched with a hint of what reminded him of maple syrup, another American delicacy that Gavin's father had allowed him to taste.

He found the girl staring at him, her expression one of expectation. He'd recognized her beauty at the inn, but here, with the early morning sun on her hair, he found her breathtaking.

"Well? Do you like them?" she asked.

He nodded. "*Ye* hae one."

"Me? Why?"

He smiled. "Because then I'll know what your lips taste like."

She blushed. "Oh, sir. You're a rapscallion."

He put his hands on his chest. "Me? Na. Ye just inspire me tae be honest."

"I suppose that's a good thing."

"So, tell me this. Dae ye always bring strange men treats?"

"Certainly not."

"Sae ah'm special?"

She smirked and looked away, peering into the sky, her hand shading her eyes. He watched the amusement on her countenance evaporate in the morning sun.

"I've got to go," she said.

"Noo?"

"Yes. I'm sorry. I shouldn't have lingered. I need to get the bread back to my father. He's waiting for me."

She offered a wave and scurried away as he leapt to the front of the shop to watch her go.

Climbing into a black carriage with extravagant gold scrollwork on the door, she paused to glance his way and flash a smile.

He grinned. "Come visit any time," he called after her.

"Who are ye talking tae?"

Broch turned to find Gavin standing behind him. "Na one."

"That was the girl from the inn last night, wasn't it?"

Brochan shrugged. "She wanted a cost on a set of horseshoes."

"Be sure to up yer asking. She's rich."

"Aye?"

"Well, nae as rich as me. But word is her da made a penny in America."

Brochan mulled over this. "Did ye ever hae a pecan?"

"Huh?"

He shrugged and turned to his work. "Never mind."

"She'll be at my da's dance tomorrow if ye fancy her."

"Wha? Fiona will? Howfur?"

"She's friends with one of the lassies wha's friends with mah sister. That's how come she stuck in mah head."

Broch scowled. "Whit dae ye mean, *stuck in yer head?*"

"Ah overheard the lassies talking aboot her, blethering aboot a new friend with gorgeous hair and blue eyes." He flounced his hair in a feminine fashion to pantomime how much the girls had gushed. "Obviously, it's her."

"Aye. Go on."

"It seems this lassie's da is hard. The sort of mad

brute only America kin make. But he'll be oot of town the night of the dance, so they've hatched a plan tae bring her along."

"Ye dinnae say."

"I dae say. Should ah take that as a confirmation of yer invitation? Will this be the first time ye grace us with yer presence at one of da's balls?"

Broch shrugged. "Ah dinnae hae the clothes fer it."

"Ah'll lend ye some."

Brochan peered down at his much shorter friend. "Yer clothes? Ah'd look lik' Hannibal's elephant dressed in trousers."

"Ah'll lend ye da's. Ah took after mah maw. That's why ah'm so *pretty*."

He framed his face with his hands and Broch rolled his eyes.

Gavin punched him on the arm. "If ah find ye clothes, ye promise tae come. Aye?"

Broch grimaced. "Aye. If ye can find me clothes—proper clothes—ah'll come tae yer party."

Gavin smiled. "Consider it done."

CHAPTER SIXTEEN

Six-year-old Toby Crane huddled in the corner of the windowless room and wiped his forehead against his *Transformers* t-shirt. It was hot. The floor and walls of the dark room were covered in mattresses and a standing fan balanced on one of them, its cord threading through a tiny hole in the wall. He'd inspected the hole, tried to call through it, but the cord nearly plugged the space.

So hot.

The fan moved the air but there was no vent, only a small cut in the ceiling, the same size as the fan cord-hole. That hole provided him his only light. The sun looked like a laser streaming through to the mattress below. He'd played with it for a while, running his hand through the beam.

Mostly he cried.

One end of the box-like room had a cutout that looked like a door, but it couldn't be opened from the inside. Pillows were glued to that spot, whereas mattresses ran along the rest of the walls.

An empty bucket with a lid sat in the corner. Toby had thought about peeing in it, but he wasn't sure that's what it was for. He was scared that if he used it as a toilet it might anger the man who'd brought him to this place.

He wouldn't be able to wait much longer.

Toby was exhausted from crying. At first he'd cried from fear. Then, something inside him said that if he cried long and hard enough, someone would come to return him to his father. When that didn't work, he'd fallen asleep, only to wake up with his eyes swollen and his throat dry and sore.

The air had been cooler and the room darker when he fell asleep. Now, it was hot again.

He jumped at the sound of a metal clanging and realized it was the sound of a latch. The pillow-door creaked opened and a long, thin arm pushed a gallon of water onto the mattress in front of the door.

It was a lady's arm.

"Let me out! I want to go home!" he screamed, crawling on his hands and knees towards the door. The lady tossed in a white plastic bag and slammed shut the door.

"Let me out!"

A panic built in his chest. He banged on the padded door.

Pushing aside the water, he grabbed one of the pillows padding the door and peeled it away by hanging all his weight from it. The fabric tore and stuffing rained to the ground.

Exposing the metal of the door, he banged his fists against it. Impressed by the noise, he continued, demanding to be set free.

Maybe the lady doesn't know I'm in here. She didn't see me.

His arms had nearly tired when the door jerked open and he fell forward onto the dirt, skinning the palms of his hands. He yipped in surprise and pain. Large hands grabbed him around his chest and a cloth covered his face.

A man's voice hissed in his ear. "You think you're smart? You think you're funny making all that racket?"

He tried to wriggle away but the man pressed his face harder into the cloth and everything went black.

CHAPTER SEVENTEEN

Brochan awoke at nine-thirty, surprised to find Catriona hadn't gathered him for work. He'd been up late, skulking around Owen's house and talking to Asher. Without enjoying a drop of Scotch, he felt vaguely hungover. Which reminded him—

Ask Catriona aboot Scotch fae the apartment.

Might be nice to have a nip or two, now and again.

A sweet, brown-sugar scent reached his nostrils and his gaze settled on the mess of pecan pie sitting beside his bed.

Pecans.

His fertile dreamlife still had the tendrils of an illusion weaving through his brain. He'd been roaming nineteenth century Edinburgh once more, without ever leaving his bed.

Probably. He wasn't sure what was real anymore.

Fiona. Pecans. Something aboot a dance...

Rubbing his hands over his face, Broch stretched his neck, both grateful and worried that Catriona had left him to sleep. On one hand, he wanted to avoid her. Her presence confused him. He hoped his memory would soon return and he would know, once and for all, if he'd left behind a lover.

On the other hand, he couldn't deny his feelings

for Catriona. He *wanted* to be near her. The feelings she inspired in him were like no other—with the exception of his dream love.

Fiona felt too real to be nothing more than a dream.

To pledge his love to Catriona when Fiona might be waiting for him—it would be cruel to do such a thing, for all involved.

From what Sean said, he couldn't go back in time to find Fiona. But he *could* investigate whether or not Owen's Fiona was also *his* Fiona. Perhaps she'd lost her memory as well. The moment he'd met her he'd felt the recognition between them.

He needed to talk to her.

Broch hopped in the shower, wrapped his kilt around his waist, slipped into a tee and took the elevator downstairs.

"Ooh. Good morning you sweet, Scottish toffee." said Jeanie, the office receptionist. She clapped her hands together and her glasses, hanging from a chain around her neck, bounced atop her pendulous bosom.

"Mornin'," said Broch, responding to the only part of her sentence that he understood.

Jeanie offered an exaggerated sigh. "I just *love* that accent of yours. Ooh! Say *top of the mornin' to you.*"

A man standing in the corner of the room in dirt-speckled clothes huffed a laugh that ruffled his large gray mustache.

"That's *Irish* people that say that, you ditz. He's *Scottish.*"

"You shush. Close enough." She dismissed the

man with a wave and stared at Broch like a child awaiting a candy. "Go on. Do it. *Top of the morning to you.*"

Broch winced. "Uh, tap of the mornin' tae ye?"

"Yes! I love it. I could just *eat* you alive." Hooting with glee, Jeanie returned her attention to her computer screen.

Broch took a stride toward the door and Jeanie sprung to life once more.

"Oh. I almost forgot. I have a message for you from Cat. She said to stick around the lot and she'd be back for you later.

Broch frowned. He'd hoped to call a car and see if he could find Fiona.

The mustachioed man placed his mug in the sink of the office kitchenette and approached Broch.

"You as strong as you look?" he asked.

Broch shrugged. "Howfur strong dae ye think ah am?"

"*Very*," mumbled Jeanie, never glancing from her keyboard.

The man scowled at her and then continued. "Tell you what. I've got about a *million* bags of beach sand I need to unload out there and my man didn't show up for work again today. Damn hippie, pot-smokin' piece of—" The man's face grew red, his volume rising until he cut short and sniffed. "Nevermind. Not your problem. But if you have time to kill, could I interest you in helping an old man?"

Broch considered the offer and decided the work might help him to clear his mind. "Aye. Ah kin dae that."

"Great. My name's Harry," The man thrust out a hand and eyeballed Broch's kilt. "You want to change first?"

Broch shook his hand. "Na."

The man eyeballed Broch's kilt a moment longer before nodding and headed for the door. "Later, Jeanie-Bean."

"Bye Kilty," called Jeanie.

Harry stopped and turned. "Will you listen to that? She's been flirting with me for twenty-five years and now she's only got eyes for you." He scowled at Broch, poking a finger. "She's my wife. You keep your big Scottish hands off her."

Broch gaped at him, unsure of what to say. They remained, locked in a stare, until Harry broke into a broad grin and slapped him on the arm. "I'm kidding. She'd never have you. She likes mustaches."

He winked at Jeanie and she threw him a kiss.

"Bye Kilty," she repeated as Harry walked away.

Broch raised a hand in farewell and stepped into the California sun.

An hour later, the sun seemed less delightful. Broch squinted at it, wiping his brow. Where were the clouds? How could there be a place without clouds?

The world has changed.

Hauling the bagged beach sand from Harry's truck had been the perfect job to keep him busy, but Broch hadn't counted on Harry disappearing. Before leaving, the old man said he'd been called to another job, but Broch never saw him receive a phone call or talk to anyone.

Without Harry to chatter to, his mind wandered back to his dreams. It drove him mad that his sleeping fantasies were appropriating his waking life. Normally, he wouldn't give his reveries another thought, but now it seemed clear that his dreams served as a bridge to his former life.

While the feelings his dream-Fiona inspired felt real, other things remained blurry. In his memory, dream-Fiona's face manifested in bits and impressions. Dark hair, blue eyes—in the end, he wasn't sure if he'd recognize her if she walked up to him and said—

"Hello there."

Broch turned to find Fiona standing behind him.

Struck dumb, his lips parted but no sound came.

"Broch, isn't it?" she asked.

He nodded. A pain stitched his left side and his hand flicked to it.

Fiona glanced at the gesture and then returned her attention to his eyes. "They told me at the office I could find you here."

He glanced at his feet. "And 'ere ah am."

She arched an eyebrow. "Do you want to put that down?"

Broch realized he still held a bag of sand clutched tight to his chest, as if he'd been using it as a shield against her. He dropped it to the ground beside his feet with a dull thud.

Fiona smiled and tossed her hair. "I don't know

how to say this, but—did I see you outside Owen's house last night?"

Broch's mouth felt dry. He opened it and closed it again, not sure he should answer.

She nodded. "I can tell by your reaction I did. You were talking to that little sycophant, Asher."

Caught dead to rights, he nodded.

Fiona rested her tongue against her upper lip and peered over her sunglasses. "Is there some way I can help you?"

"With whit?"

"With why you were outside my window last night."

"Och, aye. Ah wanted to talk tae ye."

"You mean Owen?"

"Na. Ye."

"Why?"

Broch wrapped his arms around his chest. "Ah—it's hard tae explain."

"Give me your phone."

"Mah—"

Fiona leaned forward and plucked Broch's cell phone from the breast pocket of his shirt. She pressed the button and then glanced at him. "No password?"

"Nae."

She clucked her tongue. "You should be more careful. There." She slid the phone back into his pocket, easing the edge down his chest more slowly than the alacrity with which she'd snatched it.

"I sent myself a message. I'll send you back my address. You can come by my place tonight."

"Owen's?"

She scoffed. "No. *My* place. Owen is—" she stopped and appeared to gather her thoughts, her expression of agitation slowly melting into a relaxed smile. "Owen is going through a difficult period and feels his time is better spent with the mother of his missing child as they work towards his return."

Broch nodded. "Ah see."

"See you tonight." She spun on her heel and strode away, heels clicking on the pavement.

Broch retrieved the sandbag at his feet and stood rooted to the spot, hugging it to his chest.

CHAPTER EIGHTEEN

Catriona awoke to the sound of her phone ringing. Fumbling for it, she answered.

"We have a lead on Owen's boy," said Sean's voice.

She peered at her phone to find it was four seventeen a.m. and groaned.

"What's wrong?" asked Sean.

"Had trouble sleeping and it's an ungodly hour of the morning."

"Justice never sleeps."

"Right. I forgot. So, what are you saying about Toby? They found him?"

"No, but they found evidence of him. Someone walking their dog heard noise coming from a shipping container out near Lake Arrowhead. They were spooked by a man before they could investigate, but they reported it. By the time the police arrived, Toby was gone."

"Oh, that's terrible. So *close*. At least we know he's alive."

"Or *was*."

"Mm. Any leads on where the kidnappers might have moved him?"

"Cops found a bag full of convenience store food

and a mug, a water jug, a bucket—they're running prints on everything. I've got someone inside who will let me know as soon as they know anything."

"Good."

"I thought we could go to the scene and see if anything rings a bell."

Catriona scowled. "Aren't you supposed to be resting?"

"I'm driving there, not *jogging*. Come on, it'll be fun. Like old times, working the case together—"

"Fine, fine. Sounds good. Pick me up in twenty? I'll meet you outside the studio."

"See you there."

Catriona hopped out of bed and ran through an abbreviated version of her morning routine. The shower had hot water, so she surmised she'd beaten Broch to it.

Kilty.

She'd almost forgotten he was officially her new partner.

Should I wake him?

Sean didn't mention him. The Highlander had been cranky the night before and she'd heard the elevator running after midnight. Where had he gone?

Something was up with him.

She decided to let him sleep. Driving to Lake Arrowhead wasn't a teachable moment. Neither was a kidnapping investigation. As a rule, abduction wouldn't be part of Broch's studio job description. Toby's disappearance was a once in a lifetime tragedy for the Parasol Pictures extended family.

Hopefully.

Catriona grabbed her phone, the case of which held her license and credit card, and headed outside.

A few minutes later, Sean's truck rolled to a stop in front of the studio gates and she hopped inside.

It was a two hour drive to the spot where the police had found evidence of Toby Crane's imprisonment. That was one thing Catriona didn't like about California—nothing was ever close.

"Where's Broch?" asked Sean.

"I decided to let him sleep."

"Why?"

"Why not? What's the matter, do you miss him?"

Sean chuckled. "Oh boy. What subtext is running here that I can't read?"

"I'm sure I don't know what you mean."

"There you go again. I detect *attitude*."

Catriona dragged her finger along the top of the door, considering if she wanted broach the subject of her petty jealousy. She decided to fess up.

"Fine. I might be a little jealous that he's your *real* son."

Sean chuckled "That doesn't change the way I feel about you."

"I know. But you're the only dad I've got. He just showed up and co-opted you."

"I wouldn't think you'd mind. After all, you've always called me *Sean*, not *Dad*."

"That's your fault."

"How so?"

"You told me to call you *Sean* when you found

me. Remember?"

He cocked his head. "Did I? I guess I was a little freaked out about adopting you."

"Emotionally, or because you did it illegally?"

"Both. Definitely both. Little girls aren't like puppies. You can't just keep them when you find them. People frown on that."

Catriona chuckled. "And you couldn't lock me in a room covered in newspaper when I got annoying, either."

"That was the worst part."

Catriona stared at him, debating, until Sean felt her gawking at him.

"What?" he asked.

"Nothing."

"Spit it out."

She twisted to face him. "Has Broch said anything to you about me?"

Sean held up a hand. "Oh no. I know that tone, too. If you two are going to start a romance, don't pull me into the middle of it."

"It's not *that*." Catriona traced a figure-eight design on her thigh with her fingertip, searching for the right words. "I mean it *is*. Maybe. I don't know. It seemed like things were heading in that direction, and then yesterday, all of a sudden, he got weird."

"Weird, how?" Sean shook his head. "I can't believe I just asked that. I *just* told you I don't want to be involved."

"Too late. Weird like...*I don't know*. Like his mind is a million miles away and he wants to be left alone with his thoughts."

Sean shrugged. "The man wakes up and he's three hundred years from home. He's probably trying to find his bearings. What he's been through—it would be like you popping up in the world of *Star Wars* and having to find your way."

"Would I get a lightsaber?"

"Maybe. But think about it—everything would be foreign. You'd have no family or friends—"

"He's got you."

"Sure, but I'm not what he's used to. He's got *you*, too, as a friend, I hope, even if things are *weird*."

Catriona hooked her mouth to the side. "Sure, but—"

"Just be patient with him. *Be* his friend. If nothing else develops, that's fine, too."

Catriona huffed a laugh. "Oh I *know* that's fine. I'm nearly thirty. I'm too used to doing whatever I want, *when*ever I want. I'm a lost cause."

"Oh don't say that. I'm sure there's someone out there looking for a royal pain in the ass."

"Hey!" Catriona slapped his arm and Sean laughed.

Chuckling, she put her hands over her heart and lifted her chin to stare at an imaginary moon. "Fine. I promise to keep the hope of true love eternal in my heart."

"That's my girl."

"Aww, *your girl*. That's one thing I've got going for me. I guess Broch can't ever be *your girl*."

Sean shrugged. "We are in L.A. Don't ever say

never."

They reached the coordinates given to Sean by his police contact and drove across a large stretch of barren land dotted with piles of concrete blocks and other building materials. They parked beside an old shack, its door secured with yellow crime tape. The police had left, but tape also secured the door to a metal shipping container located behind the shack.

"Not much to see here," said Catriona, exiting the truck. She peered through the window of the shack and found it empty but for a folding cot. It seemed anything small enough to carry had been bagged and taken by the police.

Planting her hands on her hips, Catriona examined the scrub brush and dirt. "Gives me the shivers to think that poor kid was kept out here."

Sean shielded his eyes with his hand and swept his gaze across the desolation.

"I knew there wouldn't be much to see. I just *wanted* to see it. Get a feel for it. You never know what experience might trigger a useful thought down the road."

"Any leads on who owns the land?"

"A development corporation planning a strip mall project. Progressicon is the name I think."

Catriona caught a glimpse of something blue in the dirt and bent to pick it up. It was a flat, teardrop-shaped piece of plastic. It didn't belong, so she slipped it in her pocket.

They spent some time wandering the area and then drove into Lake Arrowhead. It was the closest town to the container, so they inquired at the restaurants and stores if anyone had noticed any newcomers. Most commented that the police had already questioned them and none had anything new to share.

After grabbing a donut, Sean drove back and dropped Catriona off in front of the studio.

"Any big plans today?" she asked Sean as she hopped out of the vehicle.

"Nah. I have to meet Luther in a bit."

She rested her elbows in the truck's open window. "I think I'm hungry again. I was considering asking you to lunch."

"Can't today. Sorry."

Pouting, she forced her lip to quiver for comical effect. "I bet you'd go to lunch with *Broch*."

He rolled his eyes. "Very funny. Why don't *you* go to lunch with Broch and find out what's eating him?"

She clucked her tongue, stepping back as Sean waved and drove away. Strolling toward her apartment, she retrieved her phone.

Maybe Sean is right and what Kilty needs is a friendly ear.

She dialed Broch's number. As the phone rang in her ear, to her right she heard the movie theme from *Braveheart*, the tune she'd set Broch's phone to play. She changed her course to head for it.

Rounding a storage shed, she found Broch standing at the back of a pick-up truck. The truck's bed was half-filled with bags of sand, with more stacked high in the shed.

Broch stood shirtless in his kilt, sweating in the

early afternoon sun. The scar left from the wound he'd had when she first found him passed out on the lot, seemed angrier then when last she'd seen it. It glowed red above his left hip, and she wondered if it had become infected and reopened.

Oblivious to her arrival, he tilted back his head and poured the contents of a water bottle over his face and body. Rivulets of water ran down his pecs and dripped onto his stomach muscles, creating glistening paths that led into the waistband of his kilt.

Oh come on.

He wiped his face with his unworn tee, noticing her presence as he did.

"Harry roped you into doing this?" she asked.

Broch scowled. "Aye. Did he play me the fool?"

"Let's just say he hasn't done a full day's work since nineteen ninty-nine."

Broch chuckled. "Och. No matter. It felt good to work." He reached for his phone which was perched on the bed door of the truck.

"That was me calling."

He nodded and set the phone back down. Cracking open another bottle of water he chose to drink this one, rather than spill it down his skin.

Pity.

She eyed the truck. "Did you drive this here?"

He shook his head. "Na. Harry did whin he brought me water. Said we needed tae fill it and then disappeared again."

She chuckled. "I told you. Man's a genius at avoiding work."

Broch finished the bottle and wiped his mouth. "Ye dinnae wake me this mornin'?"

"Huh? Oh. No. Sean called me early and there didn't seem any point. They found where the kidnappers kept Toby and he wanted to check it out."

Broch perked. "They found the laddie?"

"No. Just where his abductors were keeping him. They've moved him since."

"Ah. That's tae bad."

A silence fell between them, until Broch dipped to grab another bag and Catriona remembered her plan.

"Do you want to go to lunch?" she asked.

He straightened, two sandbags piled in his arms. "Noo?"

"Well, when you're done. Are you almost done?"

He surveyed the remaining bags of sand in the shed. "Uh..."

Catriona's phone rang and she held up her index finger, asking him to hold his response, as she turned away to answer. It was Noseeum, sharing an update on an actor who'd cut his finger filming an action scene. No permanent damage. No lawsuit imminent.

She thanked him, disconnected and noticed a message alert. Clicking on it, she found the receipt for a car service the night before. The car had traveled from the studio to near Owen Crane's home and then later, another car from West Third St. back to the studio.

She turned to Broch.

"Did you go out last night? In a car?"

His eyes grew wide. "Ye saw me?"

"I—" It occurred to her that he had no idea her phone app tracked car usage. Maybe it was better to keep the source of her knowledge a secret.

She groaned internally.

I sound like a psycho ex-girlfriend. Why would I need to keep tabs on him?

She struggled with the decision. They weren't actually dating. There was no reason to distrust him— except, of course, he *had* appeared mysteriously on the studio lot and was now stitched into her and Sean's life...

It would only be responsible to keep tabs on a new worker. Right?

She nodded. "Someone saw you."

There. That's vague enough to not be a lie. Someone had to have seen him somewhere at some point.

"Oh. Aye. Ah did call a car," he admitted.

"Where'd you go?"

There I go again. I know where he went and I'm testing him. I have trust issues. I should speak to someone about that.

"Owen's house."

"After midnight? Why?"

He grimaced and looked away. "Ah needed to see Fiona."

"Fiona? Owen's girlfriend? Why?"

"Ah think ah've been dreaming aboot her."

A flash of butterflies fluttered in Catriona's stomach.

Stop that, silly girl.

"Okay...what does that mean, exactly?" she asked,

after taking a moment to assume the most blank expression she could muster.

Broch sighed. "Ah've been havin' dreams aboot a lassie, back in another life—"

"In the past?"

"Aye. Ah think she's Fiona."

"Why would you think that?"

"Her name."

"You think a girl you knew in the seventeen hundreds is here, dating Owen Crane, just because she has the same name?"

"Ah think it's eighteen thirty-three when ah met her. That's what she said in mah dream."

"You said it was seventeen-forty-five last you remember before coming here."

He shook his head. "Ah don't understand it."

"So—" Catriona stood, her mouth open, unsure of what to say. "What were you doing last night? Did you talk to her? Is she who you thought she was?"

"Nah. Ah dinnae speak tae her. She was inside with Owen and ah—" He cut short, wincing.

"You stared in her window but never knocked?"

He cast his eyes downward. "Aye."

"So, you took a car to *stalk* her." Catriona looked away, trying to decide where all this information might lead.

Can this guy and everything around him get any weirder?

Broch was officially an employee of Parasol Pictures now. Her duty was clear. She had to protect the studio.

"Did anyone see you?" she asked.

147

"Asher found me."

"Who the hell is Asher?"

"Owen's assistant. She works fae Fiona as well. Her first name is Kelly bit she says folks call her Asher."

"Have I met her?"

"She came as we were leaving Owen's house, after the kidnapping."

"She did?"

"Brown hair, aboot here." He hovered a hand over his shoulder.

Catriona thought about their time at Owen's and recalled the girl with a notebook hurrying into the house as the police arrived.

"Asher caught you loitering outside Owen's house staring at Fiona?"

"Aye."

"Great. I'll be looking forward to that lawsuit. Anything else I should know?"

"She gave me pecans."

"What? Is that some kind of weird Scottish metaphor for stuff I don't want to know?"

Broch scowled. "Ah dinnae think sae. Ah had pecan pie with Asher and it made me remember that Fiona gave me pecans, back afore."

"Fiona gave you *pecans* so you're going to follow her through time like a lost puppy."

Broch grimaced and seemed upset. "Ah think ah loved her," he blurted.

Catriona stared at him and he shook his head as if trying to rid his brain of something.

"Ah'm sorry, Catriona. Ah kin feel it. Ah dinnae ken how fur tae explain it tae ye."

Catriona felt the butterflies in her stomach rise into her chest, threatening to choke off her breath. She took a deep breath to blow them back down. "How would it be possible that she's here?"

"Ah dinnae ken. How is it possible ah'm 'ere?"

"Wouldn't she have recognized you if she was your long, lost love?"

"Mibbie she's lost her memory lik' me." He slapped his hand to his chest and took a step toward her. "Ye have to understand. If ah hae a love ah've lost, ah can't— I mean, ah hae tae—"

Catriona took a step back. "It's fine. Do what you have to do."

She turned and walked toward her apartment. He called out to her, but she raised a hand and kept walking. "Get Noseeum to look at that wound, too," she called back, cutting his protestations short.

Catriona returned to her apartment, where she took a quick shower before sitting at her computer.

Work.

Work she knew. Work never let her down.

A quick Internet search confirmed Progressicon Inc. did own the land where the shipping container had been found, as Sean had suggested.

Catriona navigated to a website she occasionally used—a job request board for hackers.

Would like complete employee list of Progressicon, Inc.? ASAP.

An offer popped up.

One day. $200.
She accepted.

CHAPTER NINETEEN

Broch sat on the edge of his bed, his head hanging, a white towel wrapped around his waist. He couldn't stop thinking about how he had upset Catriona. He was so distracted that he'd taken a *quick* shower after working for Harry. Things were bad if even a shower couldn't make him feel better.

He pictured Catriona walking away from him, her hand in the air, dismissing him. The whole time they'd been talking about Fiona, all he'd wanted to do was grab her and hug her. Kiss her. Go to lunch with her. Take her back to his room...

Explore this big new world with her.

Standing, he stretched, his arms sore from the day's work, and wandered to his phone. A message hovered on it—an address and a time.

Fiona's address. Seven o'clock.

He toweled his hair.

This is it.

By the end of the evening, he would know. Certainly he couldn't be in the same room with the woman and not *know* if she was the woman of his dreams?

He began to fold his kilt and then tossed it aside to instead grab his jeans. He didn't want to draw attention to himself tonight. He wanted to disappear.

When he was ready, he walked into the hall and paused before Catriona's door.

It felt like a betrayal to walk past it.

Gritting his teeth, he pushed on and entered the elevator. Outside, he called a car and gave the driver Fiona's address.

When the car pulled to a stop outside Fiona's home, he found it difficult to exit.

"You gonna get out?" asked the driver.

"Aye. Sorry."

With a stiff nod to the driver, Broch stepped out and made his way up a cement driveway to a tall, boxy home.

He took a moment to brace his nerves and knocked.

Fiona answered wearing a dark skirt and diaphanous top. Through it, he could see she wore what Catriona had told him was a *bra*. In his mind's eye, he recalled catching a glimpse of Catriona wearing a bra, standing in front of the bathroom mirror in their Tennessee hotel, fixing her makeup.

He smiled at the memory.

"What was that cheeky little grin?" asked Fiona, stepping back and motioning for him to enter.

Embarrassed, he shook his head. "Och, nothing." He walked past her, the sound of soft music tickling his ears.

"Have a seat. Can I get you a drink?" she asked.

Broch sat on the sofa. "Aye. Scotch?"

She walked to a bar embedded in the wall at the

end of the room. "I guessed that. I bought some just for you today. Neat?"

"Whit?"

"Do you want ice in it?"

"Oh, na."

She poured three fingers into a heavy-bottomed glass and handed it to him. "It's Macallan. I hope you like it. The guy at the store said it was a good one, and I would hope so, for the price."

He took a sip. "Aye. Thank ye."

"Thank ye." She chuckled and poured herself a glass of red wine before sitting beside him.

He swallowed. There was something about having her so near. She was *familiar* but he didn't feel at home. He felt confused.

"So you're straight from Scotland?" she asked.

He nodded. "Directly."

He finished his Scotch and she peered at his empty glass, eyebrows raised with what appeared to be amusement. "Let me get the bottle for you."

She stood and retrieved the bottle, pouring him another before setting the bottle on the table.

He finished another shot and set down the glass. Wiping his mouth with the back of his hand, he took a deep breath. "Ah'm sorry. Ah'm nervous."

"Nervous? Of me?"

"Fiona, ah need to ask ye somethin'—"

"What?"

"Dae ye think there's a chance that we knew each other a long time ago?"

She squinted, her attention unwavering, as if she

was trying to read his mind through his eyes.

"Do you remember me?" she asked, her voice barely above a whisper.

Broch's nerves jangled.

"Ah think ah do," he said.

"What do you remember?"

"Ah dinnae ken, exactly..." He chewed his lip. "Ah've been having dreams about you—"

"Dreams?"

"We were in Scotland. In eighteen thirty-three. And—" He cut short, frightened to say the words.

"And?" she prompted.

"And we were falling in love."

The corner of Fiona's lip curled into an almost imperceptible smile. She leaned back and took a sip of wine, staring at him over her glass.

"Eighteen thirty-three, you say? That's very specific, Brochan."

"Ye blethered the date. In mah dream."

"Did I?"

"Aye. We were on horseback then. Another time, we met at an inn. Ye were with yer da."

She paled. "My father?"

"Aye. Dae ye remember?"

"In eighteen-thirty-three Scotland?"

"Aye."

"That's crazy," she said, her eyes drifting.

"Aye."

"Wait here a moment." Fiona walked out of the room and he heard the sound of her walking up the stairs. He poured himself another shot and downed it.

Ah'm not learning anything.

For one moment, Fiona had seemed on the verge of admitting she remembered him, too. The next, she'd looked at him as if he were mad.

Mibbie ah should leave.

He was about to spring from his seat when she returned and topped off her wine.

"Let me get you another." She hefted the Scotch bottle and poured.

He took and drank it, returning it to the table with a bang louder than he intended.

She jumped, but appeared more entertained by his expression of frustration than frightened.

"Dae ye remember? Ah hae tae ken," he said. He could feel his jaw muscles tensing with frustration.

Fiona's eyes flashed. "Oh my. You're angry, now. Tell me, what about Catriona? Aren't you two—"

He looked away. "Ah... dinnae want tae talk aboot her."

Fiona laughed, seemingly for no other reason than to cut the tension. "This has grown intense quickly, don't you think? Let's get to know each other for a moment."

He released his bunched shoulders. "Will blethering—talking—help ye remember?"

"Talking always helps."

"Then aye."

"Tell you what—let me show you around the house. Would you like to see the outside?"

He expelled a breath and tried to give in to the moment. His head felt vaguely fuzzy. She poured him another and handed it to him, even as he made a mental note to slow his nervous drinking. "Uh, aye."

She stood and he followed her to the backyard. It was a small, fenced patch of grass with an orange tree in one corner and a brightly colored shed in the other.

"Have you been working for Sean long?" she asked.

"Na. A fortnight."

She giggled and placed a hand on his bicep. "I do so love the way you talk."

He glanced at her hand. Her calculating aura had been replaced by an almost schoolgirl-like innocence.

Is she flirting with me?

He took another sip. "Uh, howfur ye? Hae ye been here long?"

"Fifteen years or so."

He nodded, realizing that meant little toward proving or disproving her existence in nineteenth century Scotland. "Wherefur did ye grow up?"

She shrugged. "Here and there."

"Ah mean, hae ye always been '*ere*?"

"In L.A.? No."

"Sae before that ye were—"

She waved him away. "Let's not talk about me. My story is boring. Tell me more about *you*. How did you and Catriona meet?"

Broch tucked back his chin. "Catriona?"

She took a sip of her wine. "You and she are dating, right?"

He shot back his glass and the yard seemed to quiver for a moment. Blinking to clear his vision, he returned his attention to Fiona. "This has nothing tae dae with Catriona."

"But there is something between you?"

He sighed. "Ah care fer her very much."

Fiona cocked her head and smiled. "Oh, that's so sweet. She seemed smitten with you. I could tell."

He took a step back, feeling off balance. "Dae ye mind if we gae back inside?"

"No problem."

They reentered the house. Feeling flush, he tugged at his shirt. "Is it hot in 'ere?"

She took the glass from his hand and put it on the table. Placing her hands on either side of his waist, she stared into his eyes. "You want to take that off? Let me help you."

He shook his head, but felt overwhelmed by a feverish flush rising into his face. He grabbed his shirt and she placed a hand on his.

"Relax," she whispered.

She pulled up his shirt and he raised his arms to rid himself of it. He heard himself giggle and felt her hands slide across his now bare torso.

"Whit are ye doin'?" he said, his eyelids feeling heavy.

"You said you were hot."

"Aye, but—"

"Do you feel better?"

She leaned close to him. He could feel her breath on his lips. Reaching up, he put a hand on either side of Fiona's face and eased her back as he tried to focus. "Ah need to talk tae ye."

"Okay. What do you want to know, baby?"

She ran her fingers along the waistband of his jeans.

Whit's happening?

He could feel himself becoming aroused.

This isnae what ah meant tae happen.

His hands felt as if they had minds of their own. They slid down Fiona's arms and he found her wrists. Grasping them, he took a moment to steady himself, and then pulled them to either side, away from his body.

She leaned toward him and kissed his neck.

His eyes closed.

"Ah—ah'm afraid ah might love ye," he whispered. His mission, to find the truth of his relationship with Fiona, seemed very far away.

Something was very wrong, but he found it impossible to care.

Fiona slid her wrist from his grasp and took his hand. "Come with me."

She pulled him towards the stairs.

He laughed at the absurdity of what was happening, powerless to stop it. "That's strong Scotch," he said, his tongue sounding thick in his mouth.

Fiona pulled him forward.

He twisted his neck to look behind him and saw the newly opened Scotch bottle sitting on the living room table, still nearly full.

Fiona mounted the stairs and he followed, tripping twice as they made their way to the second floor. She led him into a bedroom and, pulling back the covers, pushed him to a sitting position on the edge of her bed. The sheets were silky to the touch and he smiled, rubbing his hands across it.

"Fake silk," he mumbled.

Knees bent, the lower half of his legs hanging over the bed, he felt someone straddle his waist. His arms reached out, hands resting on either side of a woman's hips.

He smiled. "Catriona."

When he next opened his eyes, Fiona was sitting beside him, holding his phone in front of her face. He heard a strange ringing noise.

"Whit are ye doin?" he asked. Something about the way she held his phone struck him as funny and he chuckled.

"Hello?" said a familiar voice.

"I hope you don't mind. I borrowed Broch's phone. I wanted to ask you if you found anything about Toby today? Owen and I have fallen out so, I'm not in the loop."

"Fiona?"

"Broch was telling me but then—well, we got a little distracted and then next thing I know—"

Broch heard giggling. He was almost certain it was him.

"—he's a little drunk, so I thought I'd just call you."

Broch lifted his head, though it felt as if it weighed a hundred stone. His phone, hovering in front of Fiona's face, now contained Catriona's image staring back at him. She moved like a live person, not like a photograph.

He grinned. "Hello Cat," he said, raising his hand to wave, fingers rolling like a pianist's.

Catriona's expression shifted from surprise to what looked like shock. Something about the corner of her eyes changed, and he recognized a new emotion.

Pain.

"Nae. Whit—?"

He wanted to ask what was wrong, but his head collapsed back to the bed.

It felt glorious to rest the weight of it.

CHAPTER TWENTY

1833 – Edinburgh, Scotland

Brochan stared at the door, took a deep breath, and opened it.

Gavin laughed, doubled-over and slapped his leg.

"Ah cannae wear this," said Brochan. His arms hung in the air, flapping at his sides. The suit Gavin had lent him to wear to the dance didn't even allow for him to drop his limbs lower than half mast.

Gavin's father entered the room, his eyes growing wide at the sight of Brochan. He was a large man with a barrel chest. Gavin was built like a field mouse.

"What is this?" asked Laird Logan.

Gavin caught his breath. "Brochan needed a suit fer the party. Doesn't he keek fine, Da?"

Laird Logan shook his head. "That willnae dae."

"Ah, think 'tis wonderful. The trousers provide an impressive display of his tackle. The lassies will swoon," said Gavin, barely able to speak through his laughter.

Brochan scowled. "Ye be still, noo."

"Give him one of mine," said Laird Logan leaving.

Gavin nodded, wiping his eyes. "Dinnae worry.

Ah already hid one of Da's fae ye. 'Tis behind the sofa in that room. Try it."

Brochan shut the doors with a bang and found the second suit. When he exited the library a second time, he found himself alone. In the ballroom beyond, he could hear the sounds of feminine voices.

Gavin's disappearance came as no surprise.

The women had arrived.

Laird Logan's clothing fit his blacksmith's body much better than Gavin's, but for excess room around his middle. Laird Logan had sent one of the house maids to check on him and she'd put a stitch in the waistband to keep his trousers from falling. He still found the formal clothing awkward, but only in such a way that any formal attire might feel.

Brochan cracked open the doors to the ballroom. Perhaps a dozen people had arrived, men and women, already clumping in conversational clusters scattered about the room. The musicians had taken their places and, with a smattering of string plucks, prepared to play the evening's music.

"Let me see," said Gavin, appearing from nowhere to push the doors wider. Brochan stepped back to keep from being struck.

Gavin appraised him. "Much better."

"Na thanks tae ye, ye great galoot."

Gavin snickered and dropped into a chair, hanging his leg over the arm. "Seeing ye in mah suit has given me humor fae a week."

Brochan grimaced. "Ye haven't seen me dance yet. Ye'll hae mirth fae a lifetime." He looked away to demonstrate his disgust, his gaze drifting back to the ballroom.

A dark-haired girl entered through the main ballroom entrance.

Fiona.

"There she is."

"Where?" Gavin stood and Broch pushed him back into his chair.

"Over there. Dinna draw attention."

Gavin jumped out of the chair and strode toward the doors. "Ah'll take ye tae her."

"Na, wait." He grabbed Gavin's arm.

"Easy, man. Ah'll pretend ah've come tae blether tae my sister. Flora's beside her noo."

Gavin pulled away and walked toward the women. Brochan turned to walk the opposite way, before realizing the eyes of the girls in Fiona's group, including Fiona's, were upon him. If Gavin tried to introduce him as he ran in the opposite direction, he'd look like a fool.

Brochan followed in Gavin's footsteps, hurrying as much as he could without sprinting across the room.

"Introduce me to your friends, Flora," said Gavin to his sister as they arrived, Brochan a second behind his friend.

Flora flashed Gavin a knowing smile and glimpsed in Brochan's direction, revealing to him that the brother-sister duo had already conspired to bring him to Fiona.

"Gavin, Brochan—ye ken Maid Kerr."

The brown-haired lass to Flora's left nodded and held out her hand to be received. Gavin bent to kiss it and Brochan followed suit.

"And this is Maid Jones, visiting us from America."

Fiona held out her hand and looked away, as if trying not to giggle. Gavin took it first; and, realizing he'd missed his cue, Broch next kissed it.

"We're serving food, ye dinnae hae tae eat her," quipped Gavin.

Brochan felt his face flush and he released Fiona's hand as if it had scalded him. He glowered at his friend, who ignored him. Leaning toward Gavin, he whispered in his ear. "Ah'm aff tae beat ye tae a pulp later."

Gavin smiled. "Cheeky thing to say in her presence, dinnae ye ken?"

Horrified, Brochan glanced at Fiona to see her reaction. Her eyes were wide, but a smirk remained on her lips.

"No—he's lying. Ah tellt him ah was aft tae kill him," he insisted.

Gavin stepped in front of Brochan, put his hand on his own chest and addressed the ladies. "Ah, am, of course, Laird Logan, and ye can call this uncultured brute, Brochan."

Without thinking, Brochan punched Gavin in the arm and his friend hooted with laughter, hopping away as he gripped his arm.

Broch fought the rising blush on his cheeks. "Ah apologize—"

He looked up and found only Fiona remaining. He nodded to her, unable to find his voice.

She smiled. "Hello again. Let's dance."

"Whit?" Brochan felt panic rise in his chest. "Ah don't dance."

"Sure you do."

"Na. Na ah dinnae."

She waved her hand towards the dance floor, where men and woman swirled, hand in hand. "This is the waltz. It doesn't get any easier. It's just a box."

She took his hands and pulled him towards the floor. An older woman nearby tsked with disapproval and Brochan turned in time to see her cover her mouth and scowl. He quickly strode ahead of Fiona to lead her to the dance floor.

"Where did that enthusiasm come from?" she asked, placing her hand on his shoulder.

"Ah coudnae hae that wummin think ill of ye."

Fiona laughed. "I don't care what that woman thinks of me."

Broch grimaced and turned his attention to the waltz. He'd had some training with Gavin's dance instructor, but didn't feel confident. He felt his waistband tug and worried the housemaid's stitch would give way, dropping his trousers to the floor.

"Ah'm nae sure ah kin move lik' ah should. This is a borrowed suit."

"Is it? It fits you beautifully."

He began counting, doing his best to waltz. They glided past a large clock and Fiona glanced at it. The next time they passed it, her eyes darted again to the face.

"Why dae ye keep keekin' at the clock?" he asked.

Fiona smiled. "Habit. My father is strict about time."

"He's expecting ye home soon?"

"He's away tonight. Maid Logan sneaked me from the house for this ball. My father doesn't know. He...he wouldn't like it."

She smiled, but Broch perceived true fear in her eyes.

The music ended and Broch huffed with relief, escorting Fiona from the floor. On the fringes of the dance floor, Fiona moved ahead of him and her hand fluttered to her shoulder to adjust her dress. He caught the flash of a dark bruise near her neck.

Broch touched her arm and she turned. As their eyes met, she saw his expression and her smile faded.

He took a breath to quell his growing ire. "That bruise. Yer father? Did he—"

"Don't," she said, looking away.

He held his tongue but did not move. After a moment, she sighed and turned back to him. "It's complicated. My father and I lost someone. He hasn't been the same."

"Ah'm sorry tae hear that."

She acknowledged his concern with a nod and a stiff smile.

They fell silent, and Brochan felt his own jaw tighten as he stewed over a situation he felt helpless to address.

Fiona rolled her eyes and laughed. "Look what

I've done. You're so serious all of a sudden."

"Ah dinnae ken whit tae say tae ye."

She touched his arm. "There's nothing to say. I'm fine."

Maid Kerr approached them.

"We need tae go," she said to Fiona.

"So soon?"

"Mah father isn't feeling well." She cupped her hand beside her mouth and whispered. "He thinks the kippers aren't sitting well."

Fiona grimaced and looked at Brochan.

"It seems I have to leave early."

He scowled. "Then ah assure ye, ah willnae be long 'ere either."

Maid Kerr began to walk away and then returned. "Ah almost fergot. Maid Curran has requested a ride home. We'll take her first, if ye don't mind?"

Fiona shrugged. "I don't mind at all." She held out her hand, her stormy blue eyes staring up at Brochan until he realized he'd forgotten to breathe.

"It was nice to meet you, Mr.—"

"Brochan. Call me Brochan."

"Of course, Brochan. Man of mystery."

He grinned. "Aye."

Maid Kerr rolled her eyes. "Ah *ken* ye ken each other. Yer not fooling *me*."

Fiona smiled and leaned towards Brochan. "Apparently, we're not fooling anyone," she said.

Brochan winked. "We'll hae tae try harder."

The girls trotted away and Brochan stationed himself against the wall, watching as the small group of guests gathered to leave. A man stood at the exit, bent over and pale, a pained look on his face. Broch assumed him to be Maid Kerr's father.

He made a mental note not to eat the kippers and damned the fish for taking his lassie away from him.

Brochan studied the room until he spotted Gavin deep in conversation with another guest. He stared at him until his friend felt the weight of his attention and looked his way. A few moments later, Gavin approached.

"Sulking? Ah heard yer love had tae leave."

Broch glared at his friend. "Ah barely ken her."

"Och, bit ah haven't seen ye that happy since— well—since *never.*"

Broch slapped Gavin's arm.

"Ah'm goin'. Ah'll leave yer da's clothes in the library."

Gavin nodded. "Farewell. It's a miracle ah git ye tae come at all. Ah'll count myself lucky fer mah time with ye."

Broch slipped into the library and changed back into his own clothes.

There was no reason to stay any longer.

He left by a back entrance, opting not to request one of Gavin's carriages. It would be a long walk home, but he wanted to be alone with his thoughts.

His thoughts were much too happy to rush.

CHAPTER TWENTY-ONE

Broch's eyes opened. His head ached.

Something looked different about the ceiling.

He moved his arm and felt an unfamiliar silkiness against his skin.

Not mah sheets.

He tilted back his head to peer at the headboard.

Not mah bed.

He turned to investigate his left side. By the light of the moon shining through the long, ceiling-to-floor sheer curtains framing the bedroom window, he could see a head of dark hair on the pillow beside him.

Short dark hair.

Fiona.

He sat up and the room spun. Dropping his head into his hands he took slow, deep breaths, trying his best not to hurl.

Think. Whit happened?

He couldn't recall if Fiona had remembered him or not. Had they revealed themselves to one another as lovers from long ago? He didn't remember *feeling* the answer, one way or the other.

He lifted the sheet laying over his body and found himself in the boxer briefs Catriona had bought for him.

Not naked.

Still. Not *not* naked.

He wasn't sure what that meant.

In his mind's eye flashed the image of Catriona staring at him, her expression a mixture of shock, anger and disappointment.

Had she been here with him and Fiona?

Another pain stabbed his brain and he pressed against his temple with his right hand.

Whit hae ah done?

Swinging his legs over the side, he searched for his jeans. They were nowhere to be found. He stepped on something smooth and, lifting his heel, discovered it was his phone. He retrieved it and tip-toed around the bed, taking a moment to put his face near the sleeping woman's.

Definitely Fiona.

Her eyes remained closed, her breathing steady and smelling of vinegar.

He walked into the hall and fumbled with his phone, attempting to invoke the *flashlight* Catriona had showed him it could be. The light appeared and he used it to navigate down the stairs, intending to fetch himself a glass of water and have a think.

As he reached the kitchen, a wave of nausea washed over him.

Air. Ah need air.

He jogged to the large French doors leading to the back yard and slipped outside. Bending, hands on his knees, he fought the urge to throw up.

He lost.

Taking one long stride into the grass, he vomited. He tasted Scotch, and recalled drinking when he'd arrived.

He fought the good fight and lost once more, foamy bile bubbling from his lips. The third calling, he managed to squelch his illness.

Squatting on the back of his heels, he spat and wiped his mouth. He'd never thrown up after drinking in his life. Something had to be very different and very *wrong* about twenty-first century Scotch—

"Help."

A faint voice reached Broch's ears and he cocked his head, listening for more.

"Help me."

He stood and moved toward the left side of the fenced yard.

"Help."

The voice seemed to emanate from the pink shed in the corner of the yard. Broch walked to it and put his ear next to the door.

"Hello?" he called.

Something hit the door and it shuddered. Broch stepped back.

"Help me!" said the high-pitched voice again, this time with more urgency.

Broch pulled the handle and found the door padlocked. He grabbed the lock and twisted it until the plate it was bolted to splintered from the wood. He flung open the door.

"Toby?"

A boy lay on the ground just inside the shed. By the glow of the back light, Broch could see the child's face, pale beneath a layer of red dust. Broch scooped him into his arms and the boy burst into weak sobs.

Broch held the boy away from his chest to peer into his face. "Whit are ye doin' in there, laddie? Who are ye? Are ye Toby?"

The child nodded and reached to wrap his arms around Broch's neck. The Highlander could feel the boy's hot tears ping against his chest. He held him tighter, hoping to convey that he was safe from harm now.

Broch peered up at Fiona's bedroom window. He couldn't explain how the kidnapped boy had come to be in her possession.

For that matter, he couldn't explain how *he* had come to be in her possession.

Broch spotted the flashlight of his phone still burning on the patio. He walked to it and, shifting the boy to one arm, grabbed it.

The time glowed at him.

Three forty-two a.m.

He looked down at his boxer briefs.

Och.

Groaning, he dialed Catriona.

CHAPTER TWENTY-TWO

Sean sat in his studio office, sipping coffee from an oversized mug. On the sofa against the wall sat Luther, staring at Broch with doleful eyes. Catriona and Broch sat in chairs facing Sean's desk.

"Let me get this from the top. You got a call from Broch in the middle of the night that he'd found Toby in Fiona's shed?"

Catriona nodded. "About quarter to four in the morning to be exact." She watched Sean appraise her scowl before turning his attention to Broch. She could tell he was trying hard not to react to the implication of the timing.

"And you... You were at Fiona's house—"

"At three forty-five a.m.," interjected Catriona.

Sean shot her a glare and continued. "You were at Fiona's house when you heard Toby calling?"

"Did I mention he was wearing only his underpants?" asked Catriona.

Luther clucked his tongue. "Mm-mm. That sounds like trouble."

"Amen," said Catriona.

Sean hung his head. "Okay. Enough out of you two. Let the boy speak."

Catriona crossed her arms against her chest and

slumped in her chair, glaring straight ahead.

Broch cleared his throat. "Aye. Ah had tae talk tae Fiona about...a personal matter...and ah had a drink or tae and—"

"And he woke up in her bed," said Catriona.

"Story old as time," muttered Luther, raising his morning paper.

Sean wiped his hand down and over his face. "I thought Fiona and Owen—"

"Fiona said they had a falling out," said Catriona.

Sean's brow knit. "You spoke to her?"

"Not as the cops were dragging her away. She video-called me, earlier in the evening, *from her bed*, to give me the news and ask for an update on Toby. It was really more of a group video chat though, because, wasn't that you in the background, Broch?" Catriona turned to the Highlander.

Broch grimaced and put his hand on Catriona's arm. "Ah dinnae mind any of that. Ah dinnae gae tae her hoose tae end up in her kip—"

"What's her *kip*?" asked Luther, dropping his paper and appearing alarmed.

Catriona jerked her hand from the arm of her chair so Broch could no longer reach her. His expression grew pained and he looked away.

Ashamed by her childish reaction, she took a deep breath.

Grow up, Catriona.

"Let's get on with this. Can we please talk about Toby now?" she asked.

Sean nodded and turned to Broch. "*Please*. So, the

boy was in the shed. How did you know?"

"Ah went outside tae be sick."

Catriona scoffed and all gazes turned to her.

Great. Acting like an adult lasted a good three seconds.

She raised a hand in an expression of mea culpa. "Sorry. Continue."

"The laddie was calling fer help. He wis bolted in, so ah tore aff the lock and called my Catriona—uh—Catriona."

Catriona swiveled her head to face Broch.

My Catriona?

Her attention darted to Sean and he shook his head. She understood.

Right. Concentrate on the case.

"Pick up from there," said Sean to her.

She nodded. "When I arrived, I could see Toby was weak and dehydrated. He wouldn't have lasted much longer if Broch hadn't heard him. I called the hospital and the police. One took the boy, the other took Fiona."

Sean looked at Broch. "It's lucky you were there."

He glanced at Catriona and offered a stiff nod.

"Do you have news on Fiona?" asked Catriona.

Sean took another sip from his mug before answering. "They took her in, asked the usual questions. She claims she has no idea how Toby ended up in her shed. So far, they don't have enough to charge her."

Catriona rolled her eyes. "They found a kid locked in her shed. That isn't enough?"

"She says she's as shocked as anyone."

"Of course that's what she *said*. What's she supposed to say? *oh yeah, I totally forgot I left the kid I kidnapped in there?*"

"They haven't found anything else that says she's responsible. She claims she didn't keep the shed locked and doesn't know where the lock came from."

"So Toby hasn't identified her as his kidnapper?"

Sean shook his head. "He hasn't said she took him, no. He remembers a big man and a woman whose face he didn't see."

Catriona dropped her hands into her lap. "It has to be Fiona. She had access, motive—"

"What's her motive?" asked Sean.

"To sever ties between Owen and Amber and ensure Amber remained an *ex*. You know those two – they break-up to make-up. It was only a matter of time with that kid tying them together."

Sean put down his mug. "But why would she invite Broch in when she knows Toby's locked in her back yard?" He turned his attention to Broch. "She didn't say anything to you that sounded suspicious, did she? Maybe something that sounds different *now*, that you found Toby?"

Broch shook his head, appearing forlorn. "Na. Ah dinnae mind anything."

Catriona noted that, relatively speaking, Kilty looked terrible. He appeared as if he'd been awake with the flu all night. The dull, gray pallor of his complexion did little to draw attention from the dark bags beneath his eyes.

"How much did you drink last night?" she asked.

Broch scowled. "Ah dinnae ken. Not enough tae feel lik' this."

Sean cocked his head. "Broch, when you were at the police station for questioning, did they ask you to pee into a cup or give blood?"

"Aye. They made me—uh—in a cup. Ah thought that awfy streenge."

Sean picked up his desk phone. "I'm going to call the police and ask them to run it for everything. Maybe Fiona slipped you something."

"And here I thought he slipped *her* something," muttered Catriona.

Luther guffawed.

"Ye think she poisoned me?" asked Broch.

Catriona couldn't tell if he had missed her joke or chosen to ignore it.

Sean, on the other hand, had clearly chosen to ignore her comment and continued. "There are medicines—drugs—that can make you sleep or feel drunk. The police can test your urine to see if those substances are present." He waved at Catriona and Broch. "You two can go. I'll let you know if I hear anything else."

They stood. Luther remained seated and dropped the corner of his paper to wink at Catriona as she followed Broch to the door. She smiled.

Good old Luther.

Outside Sean's door, Broch touched Catriona's hand.

"Cat—"

She shook her head and pulled away. "Don't,

Kilty. I don't want to talk about it. You're a big boy. You can do anything you want. I don't have any right to be...cranky."

"Ah want ye to understand. Ah needed to ken if she's the wummin in my dreams."

"Judging by your apparel when I showed up, I'm going to guess the glass slipper was hers?"

He scowled. "Cendrillon?"

Her eyes grew wide with surprise. The word he'd said sounded a lot like a French version of *Cinderella*. "You know Cinderella?"

Brock looked askance and appeared to mull her question. "Ah dae. Ah mind noo—ah had tae read it learning French with Gavin's tutor. That's a real memory—not a dream."

"Who's Gavin?" She shook her head. "Sorry, it doesn't matter. Point is, I guess, that Fiona *is* your long lost love?"

He shook his head. "Na. Ah dinnae get the chance to ask her aboot it."

"Didn't get the *chance*? How could you not get—" She held up a hand. "No. You're dragging me into this again. I'm not going to act like a jealous girlfriend. I'm happy if you found your love. I am." She tilted her head to the side, reluctant to share the rest of her thought.

"Whit is it?" he asked.

She sighed. "I'll be honest—I thought maybe there was something between us. But it's not the first time I've been wrong."

He stepped forward. "Yer not wrong. Ah feel it,

tae."

"Then why would you sleep with a woman you just met?"

"Ah dinnae. Ah mean, ah dinnae think—"

Catriona felt her throat tightening. "It's fine. I have to go."

She turned away and walked down the hall before she could make an even bigger fool of herself.

CHAPTER TWENTY-THREE

Leaving Broch standing in front of Sean's office, Catriona pulled her phone and called Noseeum as she made her way out of Parasol Picture's main office.

"My house. Bring a bottle of red," she said, before Noseeum had a chance to say hello.

"Hello to you, too, Cat."

She reconsidered how terrible she felt. "Make it three bottles."

"You know it isn't even lunch yet, right?"

Opening the exit door, she walked into the California sun, squinting. "You don't have to come this *second*. Just soon. And they don't have to be *good* bottles. Just easy to open."

"Should I deduce from this that you're having a bad morning?" asked Noseeum, a touch of amusement in his tone.

She smiled. "You know what? You're rich. Bring three *good* bottles of red wine."

"What if I had other plans that didn't involve listening to you moan about your life?"

She shrugged. "Then you're fired."

"I'll be there as soon as I can."

"Thank you."

Catriona spent the next several hours scrubbing

her apartment. Cleaning was a great way to distract herself from her problems. She tried to get *really* upset at least three times a year, if for no other reason than to keep the health inspector away.

She cleaned out her cabinets. Straightened her desk drawers. Vacuumed. Dusted.

Whenever she thought she'd done enough, the image of Kilty and Fiona rolling in the stupid, blue, silky sheets she'd seen on the video chat popped to mind, and she threw herself into another project.

She was naked and in the shower scrubbing tiles—slowly succumbing to mold-killer fumes—when someone knocked on her door.

She threw on a robe and answered.

Noseum stood outside her door with a leather wine carrier over his shoulder.

She grinned. "That looks like it holds *six* bottles. Excellent. You read between the lines."

He offered her an exaggerated once-over. "Why do you look like you just stepped out of the Amazon and threw on a robe?"

"I was cleaning the shower. Naked. Duh."

Noseeum entered, his nose wrinkling. "That explains why it smells like a hospital in here. I'm having med-school flashbacks."

"Sorry."

"So you're cleaning...I know what that means." He looked down at the six-bottle carrier. "It was this, or the two-bottle carrier. Seems I made the right choice."

"You are correct, sir."

She relieved him of his gifts. Pulling a bottle of cabernet sauvignon from the carrier, she brandished a corkscrew with practiced ease while Pete retrieved two glasses from her cabinet.

"It's so nice that you know the drill," she said.

He shrugged. "What are friends for?"

He poured with a flourish and she raised her glass for a toast.

"To a clean apartment," she said.

"To my excellent taste in wine saving my job once again," said Noseeum.

Catriona took a sip and closed her eyes. The wine filled her mouth with a captivating lush fruit, touched by hints of vanilla and tobacco. "Wow, that's good."

"It should be. You went right for the finest vintage, as usual."

"It's a talent."

Noseeum toyed with the little paper squares she still had piled on her kitchen island, pushing them into a flower-like pattern. He flipped over a few of the blanks to read the letters on the back.

"Don't you want to know what those letters are for?" she asked.

He shrugged. "Not really."

Of course not. If curiosity killed the cat, Noseeum would live forever.

"So to what do I owe the pleasure of your summons?" he asked.

She shrugged. "Oh, you know. Nothing in particular."

He scowled. "Uh huh."

She sat on the sofa and tucked her legs under her. "Let me ask you something..."

"Here it comes," muttered Noseeum, finding his place on the opposite side of the sofa.

"How come you've never hit on me?"

He put a hand on his chest. "*Me?*"

She nodded.

He raised his eyebrows. "Why do I feel like you just handed me a loaded gun?"

"Seriously. I mean, is there something about me that says, *nope. Bad idea?*"

He chuckled. "For me? Yes."

She gasped. "Yes? What is it?"

"You're way out of my league."

She rolled her eyes. "Oh shut *up.*"

"It's true. Look at me. I'm a hundred and fifty pounds soaking wet."

"I've seen your girlfriends. You've had some real cuties."

He scoffed. "Because I'm rich. But *you* wouldn't go out with someone just for their money. Certainly not me."

"No...but you're funny and nice and—"

"Whatever. You never asked *me* out, either, you know."

She squinted. "I always thought of you like a brother. That would be weird."

"And I think of you like a sister."

"Really? Aww—"

He raised his glass to his lips and muttered. "A sister I'd bang the crap out of if given the chance."

She gasped and slapped his thigh. "Gross."

Chuckling, Noseeum sipped his wine. "This is about the Highlander, isn't it?"

Her shoulders slumped. "It's that obvious?"

"It's more the way he looks at *you*."

She pointed at him, nearly sloshing wine on her sofa. "See? That's what I mean. He *does* look at me like there's something there, doesn't he?"

Noseeum nodded.

She flopped back and stared at the ceiling. "So I'm not nuts."

"You're not nuts. So what's the problem?"

She sighed. "Fiona."

"Whose *Fiona*?"

"Fiona Duffy."

"The one who stole Owen Crane from his wife?"

She nodded. "Well, the one the tabloids *said* stole him from his wife. I can neither confirm nor deny. And she and Owen have apparently run their course."

Noseeum let loose a long admiring whistle. "She's like—"

"Hot."

"Uh, *yeah*."

Catriona glared at him.

"No hotter than *you*," he added, quickly.

She chuckled. "*Right*."

"Seriously. She's just all made-up all the time and you look like—"

"Like I just finished scrubbing my shower."

"Right. And she's got that bad girl thing."

Catriona took a long quaff from her glass.

"Apparently, Broch likes that bad girl thing."

"He'll get over it."

"Sure."

"We'll just drink until then."

She smiled. "*Perfect.*"

An hour and two bottles later, Catriona found herself setting up the karaoke machine she'd borrowed from the studio and never remembered to return.

"Queue me up, Elvis. I'm going old school," said Noseeum, snarling his lip.

She struggled to tug the machine closer to the wall socket. "You think *you're* old school, you should talk to Broch."

"He sings the old stuff?"

"No. He's from seventeen forty-five."

"Huh?"

"He time traveled—" Catriona straightened. *Oops.*

Noseeum stared at her, a strange smile on his face. "You're kidding, right? You don't believe that?"

She dropped to her knees to busy herself with the machine and refused to look at him.

"Cat?"

She grunted. "Hm?"

Noseeum squatted on his heels. He put a hand on either side of her face and pointed it in his direction. "Tell me the truth. Do you think that kilted beefcake traveled here from eighteenth-century Scotland?" he asked.

She swallowed. "What's that now?"

"Come on."

She wrinkled her nose. "What if he did?"

Noseeum threw back his head and stood. "Then he's a liar and a lunatic and you shouldn't have anything to do with him."

She straightened.

Then Sean is a lunatic, too.

Somehow, she kept her wine-addled brain from saying her last thought out loud.

But is that a good thing?

It would feel wonderful to talk to Noseeum about everything…

Staring into the doctor's dubious expression, she sighed.

No. Better to make that decision another time. Sober.

She grinned and slapped his arm. "It was just a joke. You know, the kilt, the sexy *Outlander* thing. It was a *joke*."

Noseeum visibly relaxed. "Whew. I thought you'd lost it there for a second."

The lyrics to *Suspicious Minds* popped on the screen and Catriona scurried to take a seat on the sofa.

She held up her glass.

"You're on, Elvis."

CHAPTER TWENTY-FOUR

Ah willnae dae it anymore.

The shame and frustration of his last encounter with Catriona made Brock more determined than ever to *end* the mystery of Fiona.

It wid be easier if she weren't in jail.

He would have to wait to speak with her again. In the meantime, all he had left was his illuminating dreamlife.

He knew what he needed.

Pecans.

Broch called a car and returned to the quaint diner where Asher had bought him his pecan pie. He needed more pecans. Perhaps with some persuading, his dreams would reveal the answers he needed, *before* they ruined any chance he had of happiness.

Entering the restaurant, he spotted Asher in the same booth they'd occupied before.

"Hey!" she said, raising a hand.

"Hey," he echoed walking to her.

"Sit down. Keep me company."

He sat.

"You left so fast the other night. Were you sick?" she asked, before taking a bite of yellow pie.

He grunted. "Aye. Ye could say that."

"But you came back for more? Bold move."

He pointed to her pie. "Ye came back as well."

She dropped the end of her fork on her plate with a clatter. "It's been a pretty crazy day. Only lemon meringue was going to get me through it."

"Ah suppose ye heard...Owen got his laddie back."

"I know. And Fiona did it. Can you believe it? Wait—" She tilted her head, staring at him. "Didn't I hear you were the one who found Toby?"

He nodded.

"And you were at Fiona's in the middle of the night?"

He sighed. "Aye."

"You said that like air being let out of a balloon. I guess you're pretty unhappy that your new girlfriend is a kidnapper?"

"She's nae my girlfriend."

"You know, I thought you and Catriona..."

He grimaced and leaned back, putting physical distance between himself and her question.

"It's complicated."

Asher's head bobbed. "I'll say. Everyone's acting crazy. A day after the kid went missing, Owen dumped Fiona. Maybe he could *feel* she was guilty. I don't know." She shoveled a large forkful of pie into her mouth, looking glum.

The server stopped by and Broch ordered a piece of pecan pie.

"He's an idiot, you know," said Asher, shaking her head so hard her long earrings swung and slapped against her cheeks.

"Wha?" asked Broch.

"Owen's an idiot. He reunited with Amber about five minutes after his breakup fight with Fiona."

"Ah heard they reunited."

She scoffed. "*Idiot.* He left Amber for a *reason.* They were *terrible* together. Oil and water. Maybe more like fire and gasoline. And now, just because they went through this Toby ordeal, they think they're in love again? I didn't see that coming."

"Mibbie they are in love," said Broch as his pie arrived.

Asher slapped her hand on the table. "That's the thing. They're *not.* You weren't their assistant, watching every fight, every *thing.* It was a nightmare for both of them and now they've totally forgotten."

Broch shrugged and stared at his pie, terrified to eat it.

"Amber didn't even show up at the hospital when they brought Toby there. What a bitch."

"Whit's that? She didn't see her child?"

"No. Owen was still there, *alone,* when he sent me away—" Her shoulders dropped. "It doesn't matter. It's his life, right? It's just that he deserves better than that cheating bitch."

She took another bite of pie and looked up at him. "You're a good listener."

"Thank ye."

"Aren't you going to eat your pie?"

"Ah wanted tae take it home."

"Oh. Don't let me hold you up. Go ahead. I'll pay

for it."

"Ye paid last time. Ah hae one of these," Broch slid a credit card from his pocket.

She waved him away. "Don't worry about it. Go home. But wait—" She caught the server's eye and asked for a box. Once it arrived, she nodded to Broch to take it. "Put your pie in there. Don't carry it out in your hand like you did last time, ya weirdo."

He nodded and tilted the plate to slide the pie into the Styrofoam container. As he did so, Asher's phone rang and she put down her fork to answer.

Broch watched her expression grow animated as someone on the other end of the line spoke.

"*What?* Are you serious? How? Wow...okay... okay...I'm on it. Thanks."

"Somethin' wrong?" he asked.

She stared at him, her jaw hanging open for several seconds before answering. "It's Amber."

Brock stood. "Did she say why she wasnae at the hospital?"

"No, it wasn't Amber on the *phone*. That was Owen's business manager calling me."

"Ah dinnae understand."

She looked up at him. "He told me they found Amber *dead.*"

Now it was Brock's turn to drop his jaw. "Dead? Howfur?"

"*Stabbed* to death. Can you believe it? I have to go. She stood and grabbed her purse. "I have to find Owen. He's got to be a mess."

Asher patted him on the arm and scurried out of

the diner.

Unsure what he should do, Broch retrieved his phone to call Catriona. It rang until he heard her voice, but when he tried to speak to her, something beeped and the line went dead.

He tried again, with the same result.

After using his credit card for the first time to pay for both his and Asher's pies, Broch took a car back to the studio.

Passing Catriona's door on the way to his own apartment, he paused.

It sounded as if people were singing inside.

He raised a hand to knock and then looked down at the Styrofoam box in his other hand, realizing he had nothing new to share with Catriona.

First, he needed pie.

CHAPTER TWENTY-FIVE

1833 – Edinburgh, Scotland

Brochan walked the long road back into town, the moon so full and bright it was almost as if the midnight sun shone just for him.

Though it was a chilly evening, his body felt warmed by a fire within.

Fiona.

He couldn't stop thinking about her. Her face, the way she danced, the way she looked at him…

The sound of hoof beats and wooden wheels reached his ears and he turned, hoping he'd recognize the driver.

The evening was fine, but now that he'd been walking a while, he'd decided it wouldn't *hurt* to find a ride to town.

A black carriage approached and passed him without pausing. He recognized the gold scroll work on the side.

Fiona's da.

He turned and stared back the way he'd come.

Och na.

The carriage taking Fiona home had to make a stop before heading toward her home.

Fiona's father would be home before her and he'd discover she'd gone to the party.

She'd been afraid of him. Of that, he was certain.

I cannae let her donder intae a beating.

Brochan broke into a jog. Gavin had mentioned Fiona's father was renting the old Wilson house. If he cut across the glen, he might intercept her carriage in time to warn her about her father's early return.

He bounded over the mottled earth toward the Wilson house. When it came into view, he saw only Fiona's father's carriage parked at the side of the cottage. He peered down the road, expecting to see Fiona's ride approaching in the distance.

The road was empty.

Hands on his hips, he licked his lips and caught his breath, unsure of what to do. It was possible she'd already made it home. She might be inside that very moment, facing her angry father.

Should he go to her? Or, would it be wiser to station himself up the road and wait to intercept her?

He batted the two ideas back and forth before deciding to creep to the small house and peer in the window. If he spotted Fiona's father alone, then he would know to run up the road.

Broch heard the commotion before he reached the house. Crouching as he approached, he stationed himself below a window and peeked inside.

Two people stood in the center of the room, a fire casting their writhing shadows across the walls inside. Jones had his hands wrapped around Fiona's arms, shaking her, his face a mask of rage.

"Let go of me!" screamed the girl. Broch could see her cheeks glistening with tears.

Her father roared, his face inches from hers.

"Jezebel!"

He struck Fiona, a backhanded blow across her cheek, and she spun away, catching her balance against a table before falling.

Furious, Broch clenched his fists. As he moved toward the door, he saw Fiona's father collapse in a chair. Fiona remained leaning against the table, breathing heavily, her palm against her cheek.

Broch paused, torn. It wasn't his place to interfere with a family during a private moment, but if the man raised his hand again—

"Is this what happened?" he heard Fiona ask.

"What are you talking about?" The man's stare locked on the floor.

"Did you strike her? Is that how it started?"

Even through the thick glass, Brochan could see the man pale. He dropped his head in his hands.

"No...*no*. I don't know what you're talking about."

Fiona took a step forward. "Father, I'm not her. You can't make me be. Not anymore."

Jones' lips pinched and the color returned to his face tenfold. "Be silent. Go to your room. You will not deny your destiny!"

"It's not my destiny any more than it was hers!"

"I said go!" He reached forward and grabbed for her wrist but she twisted it away and burst through the front door. He ran after her, tangling with a chair that he tossed aside, dashing it against a wall. Framed by the doorway, he stood watching Fiona, the girl already on the road and running.

Broch spun behind the wall, hiding from the furious man, every muscle in his body straining to run after Fiona.

"You've nowhere to go. You can't run from your duty. You can't run from me!" Jones called after his daughter.

Broch peered around the edge of the home in time to see Jones spin on his heel and returned to the house, fuming. He crept again to the window and watched the man stomp the fallen chair to bits before collapsing again in his larger chair, his body wracked with sobs.

Broch saw Fiona had reached the apex of the hill leading to the Wilson home a moment before she disappeared on the opposite side. The night was cold, and she'd run out of the house dressed only in her ball gown.

With one last glimpse at the sobbing man, Brochan bolted after Fiona.

He sprinted parallel to the road, hoping to remain less noticeable if he steered clear of the main thoroughfare. He didn't want Jones to peer out his window and see a man with his daughter, for fear it would pique him to inflict greater harm on her.

A sad melody reached Brochan's ears, mixing with the sound of his steady footfalls. He stopped, panting.

Is that music?

He scanned the empty countryside around him. He peered into the dark heavens.

The music continued.

Broch opened his eyes. His phone was ringing the tune Catriona had programmed for him. The *theme from Braveheart*. She laughed every time she heard it.

Ah wis dreaming again.

Again he'd been thwarted by the modern world, his memories cut short before finding answers.

He glanced at his phone and saw it was Sean.

CHAPTER TWENTY-SIX

Catriona heard her phone ring and tried to bury her head under her pillow.

"Go away," she mumbled.

Someone grunted.

It took a moment for the sound to register, but when it did, Catriona scrambled to a sitting position and looked to her right.

Noseeum lay in bed beside her, asleep.

"Holy—"

The ringing continued. She huffed and fumbled for her phone.

"Hello?"

"Cat?"

She looked down and saw she was wearing sweat shorts and a tee.

Relieved, she expelled a puff of air. "I'm wearing clothes."

"That's...great..." said a voice on the line.

Catriona swung her legs over the bed to sit up and immediately regretted it. She cradled her throbbing head in her hands.

"Cat? Are you okay? Are you there?" asked a voice she now recognized as Sean's.

"Yes. Please talk more quietly."

"What's wrong with you?"

She twisted to peer at her unexpected houseguest—*bed*-guest—through her fingers. "I had some wine with Noseeum last night."

"Oh. He always brings the good stuff."

"Tell me about it. What's up?"

"I have two things for you. First, Amber Crane is dead."

She straightened. "What? How?"

"The cops aren't sharing too much information but my inside man says she was murdered. Stabbed. Keep that to yourself."

"Ohmygod...when?"

"They think the same day Broch found her boy. Owen saw her that morning, but she failed to show at the hospital for Toby. When Owen couldn't reach her, he sent his sister to use his old hide-a-key and check the house."

"Oh, that's terrible. Boy kidnapped, wife killed— it's starting to sound like that family is cursed."

"Or someone has it in for one of them."

Catriona tried to swallow and found the reservoir dry. Her tongue felt twice the size it should be.

Damn Noseeum and his fabulous taste in wine.

She stood and stretched. "Mm. Awful. I'm hoping that was the bad news?"

"Depends on your point of view, I guess. They found Fiona's fingerprints all over the items found in the shipping container."

Catriona gaped. "Really? So she *did* kidnap Toby?"

"It's not looking good for her."

"The timing...that would mean Fiona was still free when Amber was killed?"

"Yes. She might have wanted Owen all to herself."

At the thought of Broch's new obsession spending her life in jail, Catriona suffered a flash of joy before she could squelch it.

I am a terrible person.

She stared at Noseeum in her bed. He'd begun to snore.

Terrible, terrible person.

"This is a lot to take in, early in the morning, with this kind of hangover."

"Sorry. Then you're going to really hate the next bit."

"Oh no."

"You need to get to stage six right now."

"*Why?*"

"Martin Winfield's attacking people with a sword."

"You're kidding me."

"No. Take Broch. I already called him."

She rolled her eyes. "Take Broch? Why?"

"Do it."

"Sean—"

"Do it."

"Fine."

"Go now."

"I got it."

She hung up and slapped at Noseeum's exposed foot.

"Get up."

He rolled over, squinting. "What?"

"Get up."

He sat up and studied the bedsheets around him before looking back at her.

"Did we—?"

"Don't be ridiculous."

He scratched his head. "I think we made out..." He looked at her, an impossibly large grin blooming. "We did. We made out. I think I touched your boob."

Catriona rubbed her face and thought back to the evening before. She had a flash of the two of them falling to the floor, giggling, Noseeum's face growing closer to hers—

"No. Shut *up*. I have to go. Take whatever is left of your devil juice and get out."

She grabbed some clothes and took them in the bathroom to get changed. Freshened, she exited and Noseeum nearly knocked her over as he ran to use the facilities.

Checking her email, she found the list of Progressicon employees that had arrived from her hacker friend. She printed it out and ran over it while she combed her hair and pulled it back into a pony tail. No names jumped out at her.

Noseeum reappeared.

"I don't think we kissed now that I think about it." He sounded wistful. "I think we *wrestled*. I think you won. But the bed—"

"I think you were too drunk to drive and I took pity on you."

He nodded. "Agreed."

They chuckled and he initiated a hug.

"One of these days I'll getcha," he said.

"I'm gonna getcha getcha getcha..." She sang with him. Blondie had made an appearance on the karaoke machine.

Grabbing her phone, he found his wine carrier.

"There's only one bottle left," he said, inspecting it.

"I was afraid of that."

She opened the front door and found herself staring at plaid. She looked up.

Broch stood there, waiting for her in his kilt and his favorite *Guess what? Chicken Butt* t-shirt.

His lips parted as she opened the door as if he were about to speak. No sound came. Instead, his attention moved past her to Noseeum, who was standing behind her. Broch's expression grew grim.

"I'm dead," whispered Noseeum, looking even paler than he had a moment before.

Catriona arched an eyebrow at Broch, daring him to say something.

"Slept at home last night, did we?" she asked, patting him on the pec as she slid past him.

At the elevator, she punched the call button and glanced back to find Noseeum still standing in her doorway, Broch glaring down at him.

"Pete, *here*," she said, pointing to the floor beside her.

Noseeum slipped past Broch and joined her as the doors opened. Broch entered the car after them. He leaned against the side of the elevator, his massive arms crossed over his chest, staring down at Noseeum.

It was an awkward ride to the first floor.

As soon as the doors opened, Noseeum offered them a nervous wave and scurried out of the building.

"You didn't have to terrify him," said Catriona as they walked outside.

Broch grunted, still staring where Noseeum had disappeared.

They strode to stage six, Catriona's temples throbbing with every foot-fall. Entering, they found themselves in Camelot, complete with a round table.

Actor Martin Winfield, age sixty-two and dressed as King Arthur, swung his sword in Catriona's direction. Though he was several feet away, she jumped back and inched along the outer edges of the stage toward the cameras.

"Stick with me," she said to Broch. He followed, still visibly flustered, but the seed of bemusement kept growing at the corner of his mouth as he watched the old man swing his sword.

Catriona spotted another actor, Don Mantooth, sitting on the ground with his back against the wall. His monk's robes were torn and bloodied. A woman hovered over him, pressing a towel to his wounds.

Only two other people occupied the usually bustling set. Aisha Murry, director of the studio's Wednesday night staple, *Knight Time*, and a camera man, his equipment pointed at the raving Martin Winfield.

Aisha eyeballed Broch from head to toe and back

again as the big man watched Martin waggle his sword at them. "Oh my. Extra?"

"Feeling more like it all the time." Catriona hooked a thumb in the monk's direction. "Don okay?"

Aisha nodded. "He'll live. Lance took a swipe at him and grazed his chest. He passed out from fear and hit his head on the ground. Most of the blood is from that. He woke up two seconds before you arrived."

"Where's everyone else?"

"I told them to take five."

Catriona winced. "Did you—"

"Tell them if they breathed a word of this they'd be fired? Yes. I wasn't hired yesterday. I'm the one who was here when Jessica Binney beat the crap out of her girlfriend-slash-assistant, remember?"

Catriona nodded. "Good. So you didn't call an ambulance?"

"No. No reason to now that Don's woken up."

"I'm going to sue you, him, and the studio!" screamed the monk at the sound of his name.

"You'll do no such thing," said Catriona, throwing him her fiercest glare. He grimaced and looked away.

Catriona turned her attention back to Aisha. "Give me the skinny."

"The short version?"

"Preferably."

She threw a hand in Martin's direction. "Man's lost his mind."

"Okay, maybe the slightly longer version."

"We found out last week that *Knight Time* wasn't renewed. Martin took it hard. He's been acting weird all week. Today, he was supposed to battle the Black Knight with Don quivering behind him for comic effect. We knew the second it started that something was wrong. It was all Eric could do—"

"Eric?"

"The Black Knight."

"Oh. Right."

"It was all Eric could do to stay on his feet. Lance was swinging that sword like he was fending back the army of the dead."

"And that's a different show?"

Aisha chuckled.

Catriona surveyed the set. "Where's Black Knight Eric now?"

"Hospital. I think he broke a bone in his hand trying to block the blows."

Catriona sighed and glanced at Broch, whose amusement was still locked on Martin. The aging actor remained in the center of the stage, waving his broad sword and ranting about years of devotion, fickle audiences, taste, manners, craft service's over-cooked roast beef and sword blisters.

Catriona frowned. This was one of those occasions where having a partner who drove and had an idea how the modern world worked would come in handy. Someone had to talk to Black Knight Eric and make sure the story of Martin's meltdown didn't reach the tabloid websites.

"Send in another. If I lose, *then* you can cancel the show!" screamed Martin. He waved his sword toward Aisha. "Keep filming."

Aisha cupped her hands over her mouth to create a makeshift bullhorn. "We're filming, Martin."

"I am King Arthur."

"Sorry. We're filming, *King Arthur*."

Catriona scratched her cheek, considering her options. "Why didn't anyone disarm him?"

Aisha sighed. "It's a *real* sword. He's using his own weapon, not the dummy. Ironically, we gave him that sword as a season wrap-up gift after our hundredth episode. It's sharp as a razor. Look at Don's chest."

Catriona glanced again at the Monk, who ripped open his robes to reveal a long, thin red scratch running from nipple to nipple.

"Look at this!" he yelled.

Catriona rolled her eyes. "Oh, *please*, Don. Sack up."

Aisha put her hands on her hips, watching Martin swing his sword. "Martin's really good. He's lived and breathed this role for eight years. Did you know he takes lessons from the same guy who tutored Gibson for *Braveheart*?"

"No kidding?"

Aisha gasped and Catriona turned her attention to Martin as a *clang!* rang through the set. Broch had recovered Black Knight Eric's discarded sword and stood holding it before him. Martin mimicked his stance, right leg back, weapon before him.

The two men squared off.

"Should he be doing that?" asked Aisha.

Catriona grunted the affirmative. "He's my new partner. Swords are his thing. I think."

Aisha squinted. "He's your partner? In a *kilt?*"

"Also his thing."

"You don't think that's weird?"

"You have no idea." Catriona chewed the inside of her lip, unsure whether she should call Broch away or not.

"Is this Highlander your best man?" asked Martin, thrusting forward. Broch blocked and reset.

"Don't hurt him," called Catriona.

"I will not give quarter!" yelled Martin.

"I wasn't talking to you, Martin."

Martin glanced at Catriona and set his jaw. Jumping forward he chopped down at Broch. The Highlander blocked the blow and spun, twisting in time to block the next slice headed toward his midsection from the left. As he did so, he kicked out his foot, swiping Martin's leg. Martin teetered and used his sword to catch himself. Broch rolled away and sprung back to his feet.

"You getting this?" Aisha asked the camera man. He nodded.

"Thinking of doing an episode where one of King Arthur's men takes on a Highlander in a chicken t-shirt?" asked Catriona.

Aisha shrugged. "We can CGI-out the tee. Or we can say he time traveled or something."

Catriona chuckled.

They watched the two men exchange blows for several minutes. It was clear to all that Broch could take the battle any time he wanted.

Aisha released a low whistle. "He might be weird,

but he's *sexy*, your partner."

Catriona nodded. "I suppose. If you like that sort of thing."

"That incredibly handsome, buff and chiseled thing?"

"Yeah. Blech." Catriona pretended to shudder.

Laughing, Aisha looked at her watch. "I've got another shoot on the other side of the lot in twenty minutes."

"No problem." Catriona took a step toward the sparring swordsmen. "Broch, can we wrap this up?"

"Aye? This is terrible fun," said Broch, blocking another blow. Martin had begun to sweat, his breath labored.

"He's going to have a heart attack. Wrap it up."

Broch took an easy swing at Martin, who blocked the blow. Broch absorbed the reverberation and dropped his sword, spinning behind Martin and grabbing him in a headlock. Martin tried to slap behind him with his weapon, but Broch grabbed his wrist before the sword could touch him.

Martin screamed as Broch bent his wrist, forcing him to drop, the steel clattering to the ground. The Highlander tightened his grip on Martin, until the actor crumpled, red-faced to the stage. He fell limp and Broch stood.

Catriona approached and pushed Martin with her toe. He didn't move.

She looked at Broch. "You didn't kill him, did you?"

"Na. Ye want me tae wake him? A good slap will

dae it."

Luther entered the set with one of the studio security guards.

"Everything under control?" asked Luther, peering down at Martin. "He okay?"

Catriona frowned. "I'm told he's fine."

Luther motioned to the security guard to grab Martin, who rolled onto his back and began to moan.

"We'll take him home to his wife. She'll set him straight," said the guard.

Luther looked at Catriona. "Loose ends?"

"Black Knight Eric. He's at the hospital with a wrist injury."

"I'm on it." Luther took a step before noticing the monk. He motioned to him. "Problem?"

Catriona shook her head. "I've got it."

She waved good-bye to Aisha and then pointed at Don, who had found his feet and now stood staring at her in his tattered robes.

"I hear you're a shoe-in for that new crime show," she said.

Don's eyes grew wide. "The detective part?"

"Sure. I mean, unless your chest hurts too much."

He grinned. "No, I'm good. It's all good."

"So we understand each other."

"Absolutely. Won't say a word."

Catriona nodded and headed through the backstage to the exit with Broch at her heels.

She pulled out her phone and called Sean.

He was quick to answer and skipped the hello. "How'd it go?"

"Good. Hey, do you know if they decided to go with Don for that new crime show?"

"I don't know. I can find out."

"Don's got legitimate grievances here. Martin attempted a free breast-reduction with a real sword."

"How'd he get a real sword?"

"Apparently, we gave it to him for episode one hundred."

"Hm. That was stupid."

"Mm."

"I'd say yes, then. Don's got the part. I'll let the powers-that-be know. How's Martin?"

"He's fine. Luther's taking him home. Broch disarmed him."

"Good. Tell Broch congratulations on his victory."

"Sure."

She disconnected. "Sean says congrats on your sword battle."

Broch grunted. "Did he tell ye aboot Amber?"

Catriona stopped. "What?"

"Did he tell ye aboot Amber being stabbed?"

"He told *you*?"

"Asher told me."

"The assistant?"

"Aye. Ah tried to call ye last nicht, but ye kept answering and then disappearing. Ah ken ye were *busy*."

She realized she'd forgotten to explain voice mail to him. It was difficult remembering to explain things that she took for granted. Grimacing, she recalled ignoring his calls during her wine karaoke party.

His sarcastic statement didn't go unnoticed. She scowled. "As a matter of fact I *was* busy."

"Ah ken."

"You *know*."

"Ah *ken* ah ken."

"You *know* you *know*."

"Ah just said that."

They both fell silent, eyes blazing, jaws clenched.

Catriona took a deep breath. "Let me try this again. Asher told you about Amber's murder?"

"Aye."

"Who told her?"

"Owen's manager called her while we were eating pie."

"While you were eating—" Catriona shook her head. "You know what? I'm not even going to ask."

They began walking again, an icy silence hovering between them like a third person.

Catriona kicked a stone. "You should probably know...Sean told me they found more evidence linking Fiona to Toby's kidnapping."

Broch frowned. "She'll be staying in jail then?"

"Yep. But you can go visit her. They have visiting days. Conjugal visits and whatnot."

"We're not merrit," he muttered.

"Huh? Married?"

"Ye said *conjugal*. She's nae mah wife."

"*Conjugal* means *married*?"

"Aye. 'Tis fae the Latin."

She frowned. "I thought it just meant *sex visit*."

He scowled at her and they resumed their walk in silence. When they reached home, he opened the office door for her.

She moved to enter and then stopped to squint up at him. "You really can't tell if she's the one yet? If Fiona's your dream woman?"

He shook his head. "Na."

She sighed. "Well, for what it's worth, I'm sorry. Sorry she's in jail and making it harder for you, sorry how things are between us. I don't want to fight with you."

He smiled. "Ah dinnae wantae fight with ye, either."

She returned his smile and patted him on the chest. They strolled together to the elevator.

As they took their places in the car, he leaned over towards her ear as the doors slid shut.

"But ah'm still aff tae murder that wee man that cam' oot of yer room," he whispered.

CHAPTER TWENTY-SEVEN

Outside Catriona's door Broch nodded and continued to his own.

"Hey," she called as he reached for the knob.

He stopped and looked.

"How do you know Latin?"

He shrugged. "Ah had a teacher."

"And you still remember it? Do you picture the lesson in your head when you want to recall it?"

He frowned, pondering how the knowledge came to him. "Aye. Ah think ah do."

"Hm," she said, and disappeared into her apartment.

Broch entered his own place and fell back into his bed. One eye open, he noticed the leftover pecan pie sitting beside him.

One more try.

He stuffed four pecans into his mouth and shut his eyes, willing himself to sleep.

1833 – Edinburgh, Scotland

Broch ran as fast as his legs would carry him after the retreating figure of Fiona.

"Fiona!"

She stopped and turned, waiting as he caught up to her. She was flushed and out of breath, her face still wet with tears.

"Yer trembling," he said.

"I had a fight with my father. I had to leave."

"Ah saw."

"You saw? How?"

"Yer da's carriage passed me. Ah was worried he'd be angry with ye and wanted to warn ye."

Her expression twisted into sobs. He wrapped his arms around her to hold her shivering body against his own.

"Forgive me. Ah cannae let ye freeze," he whispered.

She clung to him and did not pull away.

Broch scanned the area. Not far away, he spotted what looked like an abandoned cottage.

"Come tae the cottage with me. Ah'll build a fire. Yer goun tae catch yer death."

She nodded.

He guided her to the structure. Inside, they found the roof riddled with holes. Sitting Fiona on a wooden chair, he piled what wood he could find into the fireplace and, finding a flint, ignited a flame.

"I won't go back," said Fiona, her teeth chattering as she watched his progress.

"All will be well."

He leaned to grab a stick on the ground beneath her chair and she placed her hand on his cheek, drawing his eyes to hers. "You don't understand. All is *not* well and never will be. He's mad. He wants to kill us all."

Broch laughed. "Everyone?"

She looked away, her shoulders slumping. "You don't know yet. You wouldn't understand."

Broch pulled her chair closer to the burgeoning fire, but the moment he sat on the ground beside her, she slid from the chair to join him on the floor. He put his arm around her.

"Ah saw him strike ye," he whispered, his eyes locked on the flame.

"You did?"

He nodded, his face warm with both shame and the thrill of her hand in his. "Ah was keekin' through the window. Ah should hae stopped him bit he's yer father and ah..."

She rested her head against his shoulder. "Don't feel badly about it. It wasn't your fault."

He sighed. "He caught me by surprise the foremaist time. If he tried it again ah wid hae—"

"Shhh," she said and he fell silent, the turmoil in his breast easing as he felt the rise and fall of her breathing on his arm.

After a few minutes, she tilted her head to peer up at him. "I think my father killed my sister."

Broch pulled back. "Whit?"

"I have to leave."

"Noo?"

"I mean I have to leave my father. I can't go back there."

He nodded. "Aye. Ah'll run with ye."

She shook her head. "You can't. It's too

dangerous. He'll kill you. He'll pay men to hunt us down—"

He reached out, his hand brushing her cheek, fingers tracing her jaw and neck. "Yer not hearin' me. Ah'll *stay* with ye. Ah dinnae hae a choice. Mah heart tells me tae."

He could see the reflection of the fire dancing in her tear-rimmed eyes. He leaned forward, their mouths close, breath mingling until it seemed as though she breathed for him.

"I can't ask you—" she whispered.

"Ye dinnae hae tae."

He kissed her to stop her from talking.

Body trembling, she leaned into him, returning his kiss as he pulled her closer.

Fiona gasped, a sudden intake of air.

At first he mistook the noise for a rush of passion, one, perhaps, paralleling his own.

Then her body went rigid.

He felt a cold breeze surge into the room.

It happened so fast. He hadn't heard the door open until it was too late. The blast.

Broch pulled back and saw only his own horrified expression reflected in Fiona's wide eyes. Her fire was gone.

Fiona slumped to her side. Broch saw the crimson stain marring the back of her ball gown, blood still bubbling from the wound.

He'd turned her as they kissed. Turned her back to the door.

The gunshot had been meant for him.

Broch saw Jones standing in the doorway, his face white as ash.

"She'll be fine. She hasn't left, she's fine," he mumbled, stepping into the cottage toward his daughter.

"Whit have ye done?" asked Broch. He stood to intercept the man.

"She's fine. We need to go—"

Broch lunged, his hands clamping on either side of the man's throat. Jones gasped for air, fingers clawing at Brochan's grip.

Blinded by rage, the Highlander pressed harder, lifting the man from the floor. Jones continued to struggle until his eyes rolled into his head, the whites flashing like warning lamps, waking Broch from his trance.

He dropped the man to the ground and returned to Fiona. In the firelight, he could see her lips were scarlet with blood spittle, her breath coming in short raspy gasps.

"Ah'll find a doctor," he said. As he moved to find help, she grabbed his wrist.

"No," she whispered.

He took her cold hands in his. "Ah cannae let ye die."

"You must know," she whispered.

"Let me go. Let me find ye help."

Her lip quivered, a single tear rolling down the side of her face. "Don't leave me. You must know."

"Och, my lassie. Ah must know whit?"

"My name—" She took a rattily breath before

continuing. "I'm not Fiona."

"Lassie, yer fevered—"

"No." She gripped his arm. "My name is Catriona."

He shook his head. "Ah dinnae understand."

Her lips moved but he could no longer hear the words. He lowered his ear to her as she whispered two final words.

"Find me."

Her breath released, her chest failing to rise again.

"Na!" Brochan tried to wake her. He took her face in his hands, begging her to open her eyes. He kissed her, the metallic taste of blood lingering on his tongue, his lips moving as he pleaded for her to rouse, again and again, as if it were an incantation.

She was gone.

He pulled her lifeless body into his arms and held her.

"I have you, Catriona. I'll hold you safe here."

"She's dead?"

Broch turned to find Jones standing behind him.

"Aye she's dead. Ye killed her, ye monster. Yer own daughter."

"It isn't possible."

He stepped forward and Broch snarled. "Stay away fae her."

Jones' jaw set, his eyes narrowing. "This is *your* fault."

He charged forward, grabbing Broch's head with both hands. With Catriona still in his arms, Broch was unable to prevent contact.

The moment Jones' hands touched his flesh, his mind filled with visions of another life. A life with his mothers. Women in a thatched home.

The three women of his reoccurring dreams.

Broch swung his arm and felt the back of his fist connect with Jones' head. Catriona's body rolled from his lap to the floor as he stood, readying for a second attack.

The man stumbled back, caught himself against the door, and pointed at Broch.

"I *see* you," he hissed.

Broch froze, struck by the intensity of the man's declaration.

Jones took a step toward the door, his eyes never leaving Broch's.

"I *see* you," he repeated before bolting from the cottage.

Broch flexed to pursue before deciding there would be no point running down the man.

He would find him soon enough.

He returned his attention to Catriona, her body lying beside the fire, her face as white as snow.

Carefully he lifted her, her legs draped over his left arm and walked her body from the cottage.

CHAPTER TWENTY-EIGHT

Catriona flopped on her sofa. The day had not started well. It might be best to go back to bed.

Alone.

She moved to stand and noticed the hacked list of Progressicon employees peeking from her pocket. She pulled it out. It seemed pretty obvious that Fiona had orchestrated the kidnapping, but maybe the list could help them confirm it. They still needed to find the male companion Toby mentioned.

Scrolling over the names, she knew there was little chance of finding a connection. She didn't know enough about Fiona to tie her to anyone unless it said *Friend of Fiona* next to the name. And, even if she did unearth a connection, she'd have to solve the problem of how to share the list with the police without explaining how it came into her possession—

Her scan rolled past a name that made her backtrack.

William *Asher*.

The name of Owen's assistant.

Catriona recalled Kilty mentioning that Asher wasn't Owen's assistant's first name, but her last.

Kelly Asher.

Asher was a pretty common name, probably.

But what if Asher the assistant *helped* Fiona kidnap Toby?

Another thing had been bothering her since her last conversation with Broch—how did *he* know Amber was stabbed? Sean had told her to keep that information secret, and already a man, not even from the current century, knew.

What had Kilty said?

Asher received a call from Owen's *manager*.

Catriona moved to her computer to look up her studio contacts and find Owen's manager's name.

Bingo. Seth Shapiro.

She dialed him.

"Hello?" said a man's voice.

"Seth Shapiro?"

"Yes?"

"This is Catriona Phoenix. I work with Parasol?"

"Oh, of course, hi Catriona. This is all terrible, isn't it?"

"So you know about..." Catriona let her sentence hang to see how he might fill in the blank.

"Toby, Amber—just terrible. I was at his house, congratulating him on Toby's return, when he got the call from his sister, Samantha. She found the body, you know. What a nightmare."

"No doubt. So, Samantha told Owen exactly *how* Amber was killed?"

"*How?* Wait, are you saying they found the person who did it?"

"No, I mean, the sister told him it was a murder?"

"Oh, sure. In so many words, from what I could

gather. There was no wondering if she'd had a heart attack, if that's what you mean. Wait, did it turn out to be an accident, after all?"

"An accident?" Catriona scowled.

How could someone accidentally stab herself to death?

She paused a moment, figuring the best way to proceed. "Seth, I apologize that I'm being a little evasive here, but can you tell me, do you have any idea what *exactly* happened to Amber?"

"What? *No.* Why are you asking me these things? Do I need a lawyer?"

"No, no. You heard Amber was murdered from Owen, but do you know any other details? Like how she was killed—if she were stabbed, shot, beaten to death—"

Seth's voice rose another octave. "What? No. I have no idea what happened to her. You are starting to freak me out and I'm afraid I need to end this phone call."

"I'm sorry. Please, don't—"

She heard the line click dead and lowered the phone from her ear.

Okay. I could have handled that better.

That was poorly handled and *confusing*. How had Asher known Amber was stabbed if she didn't learn it from Seth?

Maybe Broch misunderstood the conversation. But, if not, who else *could* have told Asher about the stabbing?

Ah. Owen's sister. Owen had sent her to check on Amber and *she* found the body.

Catriona looked again at the sheet she'd printed. *William Asher.* The last name had to be a coincidence. Didn't it? Clearly, *Fiona* kidnapped Toby. Love made people do crazy things.

She sighed.

Why can't I let this go?

William Asher's personal phone number was on the employee list as well.

She tapped it with her pen.

"Ah, screw it."

She dropped the pen and dialed the number. A man answered.

"Asher?" she asked.

"Yeah?"

She giggled, trying to sound sexy, but felt sure it rang more *simpleton.* Clearing her throat, she dialed her kitten-voice back a notch.

"Oh, wait, you're a *man*," she said.

"What?"

"Is this Asher? The girl who works for Owen?"

The man grunted. "No. This is her brother, Bill."

"Oh. I'm so silly. Sorry about that."

"No problem."

She hung up.

Sonovabitch.

Asher's brother working for the company that owned the land where Toby was kept *couldn't* be a coincidence. Still—Fiona's fingerprints everywhere... Maybe Fiona met Asher's brother and they connected for the caper?

According to Sean, Fiona's fingerprints were

everywhere.

Catriona sighed.

That didn't seem right. Fiona seemed pretty savvy. Maybe the fact that her presence was *everywhere* was actually evidence that she had nothing to do with it.

Ugh. Wouldn't that suck.

Catriona dialed Sean.

"Tell me everything you know about Owen's assistant, Asher," she said when he answered.

"Asher? She's just a kid, really. Does a good job, I guess. Or, maybe I should say, *did* a good job."

"Did? Why's that?"

"Owen mentioned to me that he was in the market for a new assistant."

"When did he decide this?"

"The day Toby was found. He said Asher was too over the top and he couldn't take it anymore. *Clingy*, I think was the word he used."

"Might she have a crush on Owen?"

"That was my impression. Why?"

"Just a hunch—"

Catriona stopped short, her eye falling on the blue piece of glass she'd found at Toby's kidnapping site. Something tickled her memory.

"Sean, I have to go."

She hung up, even as she heard Sean pressing for more information.

Picking up the bit of blue, she rolled it in her palm. It was teardrop-shaped, like a jewel—

She closed her eyes and thought back to the day they visited Owen to investigate Toby's kidnapping.

She pictured the second police car arriving. The girl with the brown bob marching towards the stairs. Her head turned, her attention captured by Kilty's skirt.

The earring swinging...

She could see the scene clearly, as if Asher were standing in front of her now, at the base of Owen's stairs. She saw the silver earring with three leaves growing from the stem, frozen in time as it arced to slap Asher's cheek—each leaf filled with a blue gem.

In her recollection, all three leaves were filled. The gems were there, but she never saw the *opposite* earring. She rewound the moment in her head to confirm. *No.* She never saw the other earring.

Catriona opened her eyes and studied the bit of glass in her palm.

It was definitely a match.

What if Asher kidnapped Toby? What if she was framing Fiona?

But why?

Owen. She wants Owen.

That meant it wasn't out of the realm of possibility that she killed Amber, too.

Catriona recalled what Sean had told her about Owen's intentions.

If Owen tried to fire Asher—

Uh oh.

She grabbed her phone and called Owen Crane. "Hello?"

The voice on the other side of the line sounded almost giggly, and for a moment, Catriona doubted she'd dialed the correct number.

"Owen? It's Catriona."

"Hi, Cat, how are you?"

This tone was more what she had expected. Now Owen sounded like a broken man. Who could blame him? His boy taken, a relationship ended, an estranged wife murdered—Owen had endured more than one man could be expected to handle.

"I'm good, Owen. More importantly, how are *you*?"

He sniffed. "Oh, you know. As well as can be expected. Terrible."

"I'm so sorry. Look, I apologize in advance, but I need to ask you something about your assistant."

"Asher? Funny you should mention her. She just walked in."

Catriona paused. Lowering her voice she said, "Listen to me. Don't say anything Asher would *recognize* for a second, okay? Just answer yes and no. Got it?"

"Why?"

"Yes or no."

"Fine. Yes."

"Did she hear you tell me that she'd just walked in?"

"Yes."

Shoot.

"Are you planning on firing her?"

"Firing her?"

"Owen. For the love of—*yes or no?*"

"Yes. I guess."

"Did she hear you say the word *firing* that I *told you*

not to say?"

"No. I don't think so. She went into the kitchen."

She lowered the phone.

Dumbest man on the planet.

She lifted the phone. "You suck at this, you know that?"

"Cat, I checked to see if she was listening first. I'm not *stupid*. She'd left the room."

"Right. So there's no chance she heard you talking about her and then slipped around the corner explicitly for the purpose of eavesdropping on your conversation?"

There was a pause and then, "Oh."

"Listen to me. I'm on my way. Whatever you do, *do not fire her*. Be nice to her. Be sweet. Don't tell her I'm coming."

"Why?"

Catriona took a moment to consider how much information she should share. "Don't be alarmed, but I think she might be dangerous. I'll give you the details later, but there are connections between her and Toby's kidnapping. Do you understand what I'm saying?"

"Wait, what?"

"*Yes or no*, Owen."

"That's crazy. What connections—"

"Owen, for the love of all that is holy, if you don't do what I say and stop asking questions—"

"Fine."

"Good-bye. Don't say another word."

She hung up, grabbed her gun, and moved to the

door. She opened it to find Broch standing in the hall, his hand raised as if to knock. She jumped and slapped a hand on her chest.

"Gah. You scared me."

"Sorry. Ah had a dream," he said, his face split by a grin.

"Great. We have to go."

"But—"

She shut the door behind her and pulled him towards the elevator.

CHAPTER TWENTY-NINE

In the elevator, Broch tried again.

"Ye dinnae understand. Those dreams ah've been havin'—"

"Hold that thought. We have an emergency."

"We dae?"

"I'm going to tell you this like ripping off a Band-Aid—"

"A band-whit?"

Catriona's eyes closed as her expression relaxed into the calm countenance she assumed whenever he asked too many questions in a row.

He loved how patient she was with him. He just wanted to grab her and kiss her and—

She kept talking, oblivious to his growing urgency. "A Band-*Aid*, Kilty. It's a—" She shook her head, another clear sign he'd missed something. "Nevermind. Bottom line, I think your friend Asher is actually the one who kidnapped Toby."

"Why? Howfur could that be?"

"Her brother works for the company who owns the container they kept Toby in. Toby said he was taken by a man and a woman...I think it was Asher and her brother." She paused, grimacing. "Ready for the worst part?"

The elevator doors opened and Catriona immediately dropped her intense stare to stride into the office. With her back to him, he could see she had her gun tucked into the back of her jeans.

"Ye brought yer gun?"

He scurried to catch up to her as she burst from the office and headed for her truck. He walked beside her as she continued.

"The worst part, is I think Asher killed Amber Crane too. She or her brother, but it was her idea."

"How come wid she dae these things?"

They reached the parking lot and Catriona opened her Jeep door to hop inside. He entered on the passenger side and she pulled out of the parking lot before continuing her theory.

"My best guess is that Asher's in love with Owen. I think when he broke up with Amber, she thought it was her chance, but Fiona already had his attention."

Broch pondered this, recalling the little smile that Asher grew whenever she mentioned Owen. "She *did* seem to favor Owen."

Catriona nodded. "I think she might have framed Fiona for Toby's kidnapping. She wanted to rid herself of the competition."

"Bit why tak' the man's son if she loves him?"

"To erase his ties to Amber? Or maybe she never intended to actually harm Toby. She might have been setting the stage, making it seem even more likely that *Fiona* killed Amber. Making it look like Fiona was on a rampage to erase Owen's former life."

Catriona bobbed her head from side to side.

"Or...Amber's murder might have been unplanned. When Amber and Owen reunited, Asher realized Owen would never be hers with Amber in the picture, and decided she had to go."

Broch stared at the dashboard, absorbing the information. "She seemed sweet. She blethered tae much, bit she was sweet tae me."

"I don't know how it will shake out, but right now I can't let Owen be alone with Asher, and she's with him right now. He was about to fire her."

"Fire her?"

"Send her away. Cease her employment. If she even suspects that, who knows what she'll do."

"Och."

Catriona pulled to the curb in front of Owen's house and leaned into the back seat to retrieve a black, light-weight jacket. She exited and donned it, checking to be sure it covered her weapon as he joined her.

"Let me take the lead and do the talking. She seems to like you—"

"She said ah'm not her type."

Catriona arched an eyebrow. "Uh...okay. That makes sense. Her type is *Owen*. But she ate pie with you right? You talked?"

"Aye."

"So she likes you enough to eat pie with you. If you see an opening where you can lead her outside without being obvious about it, do it. I want her away from Owen, but for now, I don't want to let her know we suspect anything."

He nodded and they climbed the stairs to Owen's

front door.

Catriona knocked. No one answered. She knocked a second time and the door opened.

Asher smiled, her gaze bouncing off Catriona and landing on Broch.

"Hi, you," she said.

He couldn't help but smile back. She seemed in good spirits and he guessed Owen hadn't yet fired her.

Something about Asher was different. She wore a skin-tight skirt and a shirt unbuttoned low. Her hair was smooth and shiny, her eyes rimmed with the same black paint Catriona donned the night Sean took them out to dinner.

"Hi. I have a meeting with Owen," said Catriona.

"A meeting?" Asher scowled.

"Mm-hm. Can we come in?"

"Uh, actually, he ran out for something. I'll let him know you stopped by."

"I'll wait. It's pretty important. Where's Toby?" Catriona asked her question as she walked past Asher into the house.

Asher looked up the stairs and stepped back to allow Broch to enter.

"He took him along for the ride," she said, her words falling slowly, as if she was unsure. She shut the door and stood staring at the floor.

"Asher?" asked Catriona.

The girl looked up as if snapping from a trance. "Huh?"

"Would it be too much trouble to ask for a glass of water?"

She nodded. "Sure. I'll be right back."

Asher disappeared into the back of the house.

"This doesn't feel right," Catriona whispered to Broch the moment Asher left. "She's all dolled-up. I think she's lost it. Owen might be dead in a closet already."

Broch scowled. "Na."

Catriona's mouth twisted into a knot. "Keep your wits about you. I think—"

Broch spotted a flash of movement behind Catriona. Asher had entered the opposite side of the room. She had a gun in her shaking hand, pointed at them. Her eyes were wild.

"He left me!" she screamed. "That's why he took Toby—he was running and he left me here."

The tendons in her arms flexed.

Broch knew the truth in an instant.

She's going to fire.

Catriona stood between him and the gun.

Again.

It was his dream, come to life. Instead of Jones, Asher was the threat.

Broch grabbed Catriona by her upper arms, jerking her away, facing his back to the gun and blocking her with his body as it went off.

Catriona wrenched one shoulder from his grasp almost immediately. He flailed, reaching to keep her tucked behind him.

That's when he felt the pain.

It was as if a hot poker struck him below the shoulder. Another blast sounded, this one much closer. Catriona had drawn her weapon and fired, her hand beneath his elbow, and he felt the heat and reverberation of her pistol against his arm.

There was a yelp and a crash. His legs buckling, he pulled Catriona down with him as he fell, determined to stay between her and Asher's weapon.

"It's good," said Catriona as they hit the ground. "She's down. I have to go—"

She struggled away from him, running toward where he'd last seen Asher.

"No!" he called, reaching for her.

He rolled on his side to assess the threat. Asher lay crumpled on the ground, holding her stomach. Her gun had clattered to the floor several feet from her body and he watched as Catriona kicked it across the room.

Asher moaned. "Why? We were going to be *together*. Why would he run without me?"

Broch saw blood staining Asher's yellow blouse and glanced at his chest to find a dark pool of red darkening his own shirt, below his left armpit.

Gun trained on Asher, Catriona retrieved her phone with her opposite hand. She backed toward Broch while talking to someone. Broch suspected it was the police. Her eyes were locked on Asher, who had curled into a ball, sobbing.

"Don't move a muscle except to keep pressure on that wound, Asher," commanded Catriona as she knelt beside Broch.

Catriona turned her attention to Broch, her face a mask of worry.

"You're hit," she said.

"It gaed clean through. Are ye hurt?"

Catriona looked confused for a moment and then searched her body for damage. She glanced at the wall behind them.

"I'm fine. The bullet went through you, passed me, and hit there." She pointed to a bullet hole.

Impulsively, he grabbed Catriona and pulled her against him, his fear for her safety still jangling every nerve in his body.

"Ah couldnae lose ye again," he whispered.

Her lips brushed his ear.

"You're making it hard to keep an eye on Asher."

He released her and saw her arm outstretched, gun pointed in Asher's direction. He tried to rise, but she pushed him back.

"Stay down," she said.

Catriona placed her opposite hand on his wound, pressing him to the floor. He grunted in pain and she smiled at him.

"Big baby."

Outside, police sirens approached.

She turned and stared at the hole in the wall. "That bullet would have gone right into my head."

He reached up to cup her face in his hand. "Never. Nae wit' me here."

Her expression softened for a moment before her brows knit. "Wait. Did you say lose me *again*?"

He nodded. "Ah've been tryin' to tell ye. Mah dreams. Ah ken noo. They weren't aboot Fiona."

"No?"

"Na. It was *ye*."

Catriona's eyes opened wide.

"Me?"

"Aye. Ah was in love with *ye*. Ah always hae been. Ah ken that noo."

Catriona's lip began to quiver. She bit it and looked away. "Adrenaline. I can't stop shaking," she mumbled.

"Police!" said a voice at the front door.

Brock closed his eyes, smiling as the sound of boots on the hardwood floors approached.

CHAPTER THIRTY

Catriona winced as the emergency room doctor inspected Broch's wound, peeling back bandages applied by the EMTs at Owen's house.

Sean had driven to the hospital to meet them and now stood beside her. "Why does this all seem familiar?" he asked.

Catriona smiled. "Tell me about it. You two need to stop catching bullets." She didn't want Broch to know just how worried she was for him.

Broch grimaced as the doctor examined the entry wound in his back. He caught Catriona's eye and played off his distressed expression as if it were an aborted sneeze.

She chuckled to let him know he wasn't fooling anyone.

"Looks like you got lucky. Can't remember the last time I saw such a clean shot. Went straight through," said the doctor.

Relieved, Catriona released a deep breath and squeezed Sean's hand.

The doctor turned to them. "We're going to take him back to surgery and stitch him up. You can wait out front." With a nod he strode out of the room.

Catriona moved to leave with Sean leading the

way. She hadn't taken a step before Broch grabbed her wrist and guided her back to him. He made his intention clear and, with a quick glance to be sure Sean had left, she stepped closer.

They kissed, the touch of his lips on hers sending electricity through her body. He kissed her jaw and chin as she tilted back her head to allow him access to her throat.

"Nothin' is aff tae keep me fae ye noo," he whispered, working his way toward her ear.

She shuddered as his teeth brushed her neck.

"Shouldn't I be mad that you didn't recognize me in your dreams?" she asked.

She felt his head shake as he kissed where her neck met her shoulder. "Och, na."

Impressions from the few stolen moments they'd had together in Tennessee flashed in her memory. She ached to re-enact them. Here. On the hospital bed. On the hospital floor.

Wherever.

There was definitely something *sexy* about a man taking a bullet for you.

Broch's hands slid to her hips and he pulled her toward him to nibble her neck with even greater urgency.

A soft, involuntary moan left her lips and her legs nearly buckled. She put a hand on the side of his head to still him.

"We can't do this here. They'll be back to get you any second."

He pulled back and stared into her eyes. "Ah kin

promise whit ah hae in mind fer ye will tak' mair than a second," he said.

She swallowed.

Oh my.

There was a rustle outside their curtained area and Broch grasped her, hugging her against the uninjured side of his body, holding her until she melted into the crook of his arm.

"Ye'll be here when ah come back?" he asked, kissing the top of her head.

She looked up at him. "I could arrange that."

His mouth hooked into a smile. The curtains parted and a nurse entered with a wheelchair.

"Time to go." She motioned for him to hop off the examining table and sit.

Catriona pecked Broch on the cheek and moved out of his way. As he sat in the wheelchair, she pointed at her face.

"Before you go, take a good look at me," she said.

His brow knit. "Eh?"

"So you don't forget who I am or confuse me with anyone else."

He laughed as the nurse wheeled him away.

"Not again," she heard him call from the hallway.

Her own grin still lingering, Catriona moved to the waiting room to find Sean.

"Look at you," Sean said, watching her approach.

She scowled. "What?"

"You look *dreamy*. Looks like you two worked out your issues?"

She tittered at his use of the word *dreamy*. "Shut it.

I thought you didn't want to know anything?"

He nodded. "Good point. I was just testing you."

Catriona chuckled. "Well, for what it is worth, you could say there was a misunderstanding, but we've worked it out, yes."

"At least your love life is better than Owen and Asher's," Sean muttered, raising his magazine.

She looked at him. "Owen and Asher? You're saying they were involved?"

Sean dropped his reading back into his lap. "Seems like it. I just got off the phone with my buddy at the station."

Catrina gaped. "Ah...So *that's* why Asher was moaning that he'd left her behind. When Broch and I showed up she guessed we knew something and realized Owen had taken Toby and run—without so much as warning her."

"Asher told the police everything that happened was Owen's idea and that he left her holding the bag."

"Did they find Owen?"

"Grabbed him and Toby at the airport. They were on their way out of the country."

"Oh boy. So I guess he *was* involved? He kidnapped his own kid? Why?"

"Not according to him. He admits to a dalliance with Asher. But says, unbeknownst to him, Asher kidnapped Toby to frame Fiona and get her out of his life. Ironically, the whole ordeal brought him back to his wife. When Asher found out he and Amber had reunited, she killed Amber in a jealous rage and told Owen she'd tell the world *he* was responsible if he didn't stay with *her.*"

"If what Owen says is true and he's innocent, why did he run?"

"Said he was scared—of Asher, of people thinking he was complicit—everything."

"He didn't sound scared when I talked to him on the phone."

Sean tilted his head and raised his eyebrows. "And that brings us to Asher's side of the story."

"Oh boy. Here we go."

"*She* says the kidnapping and framing Fiona was *Owen's* idea and she was too lovesick not to do what he asked. She enlisted her brother to do the dirty work."

"Why would he want to frame Fiona for anything?"

"Asher says Fiona had some weird control over him. He was desperate to break from her but too scared to do it. Maybe she had something on him?"

Catriona considered this. "Broch said Owen broke up with Fiona. That doesn't sound like a man terrified of her."

"No, but who knows? If Fiona was interested in Broch, she might have lied about the breakup with Owen to seem more accessible."

Catriona growled. "Mm. *Bitch.*"

Sean chuckled.

"What about Amber? Did Asher admit to killing Amber for love?"

Sean nodded. "Oddly enough, she did. Said when she rid Owen of Fiona only to find him back in the arms of Amber, she snapped."

Catriona grimaced. "If Asher admitted to stabbing Amber, then I'm buying her side of the story on all accounts. Why admit to murder and lie about anything else?"

Sean pointed at her. "Bingo. My thought as well. I've recommended Parasol Pictures end their contract with Owen Crane."

Catriona shook her head and shuffled through a pile of old magazines. "Why do we help these people? They're all *awful*."

Sean laughed and patted her knee.

Catriona's phone pinged and she glanced at it. It was a text from an unknown number.

Pick me up.

Someone apparently thought she was a taxi service. She ignored it.

The phone pinged again.

Getting out of prison now. Pick me up. We have things to talk about. Privately.

She texted back. *Who is this?*

Her answer appeared.

Fiona.

Catriona looked at Sean. "Hey, did your cop buddy mention Broch's urine test?"

"Hm? Oh. I forgot to tell you. It was positive."

"So Fiona really roofied him?"

"According to her, not on purpose. They questioned her about it and she said she'd been gifted that bottle of Scotch by a creepy first date years ago. She thinks the bottle was laced and *she* was the intended victim."

"I don't suppose she remembers this creepy date's name?"

"Nope."

Catriona grimaced. "Uh-huh. How *convenient*. What should we do?"

Sean shrugged. "Nothing."

"Nothing?"

"Pressing charges would be a mess. I don't relish the idea of introducing Broch, who has no social security number or documentation of any kind, to the court system. It's bad enough he's here."

Catriona sighed. "I guess you're right."

Sean returned to his magazine and her phone pinged again.

Fiona.

Come. Now. Alone.

Catriona stood. "You okay waiting on him? I have to run a quick errand. I'll be back."

Sean nodded. "Anything I should know about?"

She shook her head. "No. The usual crap. Borrow your keys? I'll be back before they're done with him."

He fished in his pocket and tossed his keys to her.

CHAPTER THIRTY-ONE

Catriona left the hospital and drove to the jail, her mind whirring with reasons why Fiona Duffy might request *her* for a post-lockup chauffeur. Fiona wasn't under contract with Parasol and while the woman's presence *had* unduly affected her relationship with Broch, she'd only met her at Owen's house the one time. She'd watched her hauled away in handcuffs the night Broch found Toby. That was it.

I'm no one to Fiona. Why would she call me?

As she approached the prison, she spotted Fiona standing outside. She pulled up and the actress hopped into Sean's truck as casually as if they'd been friends for years.

"Thanks. I appreciate this," she said.

Catriona stared at her, unsure of how to proceed.

Fiona looked at her. "You know where I live, right?"

Catriona put the truck in drive. "Sure. I watched them arrest you there, remember?"

Fiona chuckled. "You haven't changed. You still don't know how to handle me."

Catriona glanced at her. "I don't *know* you."

Fiona's expression danced with amusement. "Oh, yes you do. You and me and Brochan go *way* back. Tell me, do you remember anything about how you got here?"

Catriona scowled. She didn't like whatever game Fiona was playing, but her training told her to say as little as possible and allow the woman to reveal herself.

"How I got *where?*" she asked.

"Hollywood. How old were you?"

"I was born here, why?"

Fiona gasped. "Born here? You remember being a little girl here?"

"Of course—" Catriona stopped short.

Oh no.

Suddenly, Catriona had a terrible feeling she knew *exactly* what Fiona meant.

She hung her head and grunted.

"What is it? Did you remember something?" asked Fiona.

"No. I *realized* something. You're one of *them.*" She glanced at her passenger for confirmation.

Fiona arched an eyebrow. "One of *them?*"

"I won't elaborate. You know what I mean...or you don't."

Fiona smiled. "Oh, I know what you mean. You just worded it incorrectly. You meant to say, 'you're one of *us.*'"

Catriona felt her stomach twist in knots. There it was again, coming from an independent source. The accusation that she, too, had traveled through time.

Maybe Fiona was right. Maybe she was one of *them.*

"Who was it who killed you?" asked Fiona.

Catriona's head swiveled so fast she nearly drove off the road. *"What?"*

"Who killed you? If you were born here, it means you started from scratch. It means instead of jumping, body intact, you left your body behind." She clucked her tongue. "Fascinating."

Fiona reached out and touched Catriona's arm as if checking to see if she was real. Catriona flinched away.

The actress smiled. "No wonder you don't remember me."

"Who *are* you?"

Fiona looked around the truck's cabin. "This is nice for a truck. I didn't picture it being so luxurious inside."

"Don't try and change the subject."

"I already have."

Catriona set her jaw. "Fine. You want to change the subject? How about this. Why did you drug Broch?"

Fiona laughed. "I told the police it was an accident."

"We both know that isn't true. And he didn't *accidentally* end up in your bed."

"No. That he did on his own. Willingly. I told you. We're old friends."

Catriona glared at Fiona, who sat stroking her own throat as if deep in thought, her long nails scratching across her skin. Feeling Catriona's gawk, she turned.

"Have you seen that beautiful wound on his

side?"

Released from the mesmerizing motion of Fiona's fingers, Catriona returned her attention to the road, refusing to answer.

Undaunted, Fiona continued. "You have seen it. I can tell. Does he remember where it came from? I couldn't get a straight answer out of him. Not healing well, is it?"

Catriona drove in silence, her face flushed and anger rising. They were nearing Fiona's house, she could see it in the distance. She needed answers.

"You said we had to talk. *So talk*," said Catriona.

Fiona sighed. "I might have changed my mind. I don't think you're ready."

"Ready for what?"

"You were always naive. You and your need to see the best in everyone. To *help* everyone."

Catriona pulled over and put the truck in park. She turned to confront Fiona.

"Why do you keep talking like we know each other?"

Fiona grabbed her bag of belongings, opened the door and swung her long legs to the ground. She shut the door and began to walk the path to her house.

Furious, Catriona rolled down the passenger side window. "Stop. Who are you?" she called.

Fiona turned and tilted her head, as if addressing a child. "Don't feel bad, Cat. You were still young when she died. When he tried to kill me."

"When who—"

Catriona felt the blood drain from her cheeks as a

memory flashed before her eyes. Her head fell and she stared at the empty passenger seat.

A tall man. A frightened woman. A defiant girl.

Fiona smiled. "Oh. Look at that. You remember. How was it after I was gone? I have a feeling Father didn't handle things well."

"He called me by your name," said Catriona, her words barely above a whisper.

"What's that?"

Catriona's eyes lifted back to Fiona, her voice stronger. "He called me by your name."

Fiona laughed. "Did he? Ouch. I *am* sorry. You know I was his favorite, of course. You took after mother."

Catriona's mind was reeling.

Fiona returned to the truck. "Don't feel bad that you forgot us. You're supposed to. Father remembers everything. That's why he's mad." She sniffed, a wistful smile rising to her lips. "I'm afraid I'm a lot like him."

Fiona placed a hand on the door and leaned into the window. Her voice dropped to a conspiratorial whisper.

"He'll find us now, you know. Now that we're together. Together, we're like a lighthouse on his darkened sea."

Fiona winked before spinning on her heel and heading for home.

Catriona sat speechless for a beat and then called out again. "Wait."

"Later, Sis." Fiona said, raising a hand to wave

without turning.

"Wait," repeated Catriona, quietly.

She watched Fiona disappear into the house.

THE END

Look for the next Kilty novel coming Fall 2017!

OTHER BOOKS BY AMY VANSANT

Pineapple Port Mysteries

Funny, mysteries full of unforgettable characters

Pineapple Lies (I) Pineapple Mystery Box (II)
Pineapple Puzzles (III) Pineapple Land War (IV)
Pineapple Beach House (V) Pineapple Disco (VI)
Pineapple Gingerbread Men (VII) Pineapple Jailbird (VIII)

Kilty Romantic Comedy/Thrillers

Funny, suspenseful romance - touch of time-travel

Kilty as Charged (I) Kilty Conscience (II) Kilty Mind (III) Kilty as Sin (IV)

Angeli Urban Fantasy

Thrilling adventures with a touch of romantic comedy

Angeli (I) Cherubim (II) Varymor (III)

Slightly Romantic Comedies

New Adult/Adult zany romantic romps

Slightly Stalky (I) Slightly Sweaty (II)

The Magicatory (middle-grade fantasy)
Moms are Nuts (editor: humor anthology)
The Surfer's Guide to Florida (non-fiction: out of print)

Thank you for taking time to read *Kilty Conscience!* If you enjoyed it, please consider telling your friends or posting a review on Amazon or GoodReads or wherever you like to roam. Word of mouth helps poor starving authors so much!

To keep up with what I'm writing next, visit my humor blog/author site and sign up for my newsletter at:

http://www.AmyVansant.com

Twitter:
https://twitter.com/AmyVansant

Facebook:
https://www.facebook.com/TheAmyVansant

For questions or delightful chit-chat:
Amy@AmyVansant.com

ABOUT THE AUTHOR

Amy has been writing and finding other creative ways to make no money since high school.

She specializes in fun, comedic reads about accident prone, easily distracted women with questionable taste in men.

So, autobiographies, mostly.

Currently, she is a nerd and Labradoodle mommy who works at home with her goofy husband.